The Prince

The weight of this crown is heavier than that of Queen Thestera's. Her crown is light weight, white gold with iridescent jewels around its rim, and a sizeable pearl at the center of the highest spear. The heavy crown in my hands is dark grey metal with no jewels and no tall arches. It is cold, thin, and unremarkable. Yet it most often sits atop the head of the most powerful being in Fenrir.

I smile at that thought.

My head is slightly bigger than Cal's, so his crown sits on top of my head rather than snuggly around it. That doesn't stop me from wearing it. My neck muscles tense to keep my head up and the crown balanced. *I can't wear that thing all day*, he's said to me. *It weighs a ton.* He explained it was something about the metal that caused it to weigh so much. It was a sturdier, more powerful and indestructible metal that caused it to feel denser than it looked. It was custom made for Cal when he was declared Prince of the Realm of Fenrir. The material was delivered to King Caderyn and Queen Thestera by two mysterious men when Cal was only a baby. That story, of course, is from Cal, so I'm not sure how much truth is found in it. I certainly do not think Cal to be a liar, but I do think him to be a susceptible child believing the story his parents told him. No matter how long ago that story was told.

I turn my head so fast at the sound of the shriek that the crown fails to the stone floor with a heavy thud. I run through the bedroom doors and toward the screams and shouts. A child starts crying; a woman screams and grunts; men shout for them to be silent. As I round the corner and gallop down the winding staircase, I spot the group of Staxeons dragging the woman and child toward the entrance of the castle. One of the Staxeons is barking at the child to shut up and keep quiet. They don't notice me until I wrap my arm around his neck and tear him to the ground, snatching the crying toddler from his arms before she hits the floor.

"Run!" I order her. She screams as arms wrap around me and tug me backward. I slam my head back into the man's skull. Another Staxeon reaches for my legs as I kick toward him.

"Take them!" One orders. "Grab the girl!"

I flip the Staxeon off of my back, slamming him onto the floor. "Run! Run to the guards!" I yell at the little girl. She staggers backward before turning and running. I grab the Staxeon chasing after her, and smash my elbow into his face. Another lifts a guard grade pistol at me. I drop to the floor, kicking out his legs before he can squeeze the trigger, and connect my bare foot with his face. His harmlessness is defined by the cracking noise and his head dropping to the floor.

I hear the woman's struggle as she is being carried out fighting by one giant Staxeon. The heavy charging steps of guards can be heard in the distance. They will have grabbed the girl, but they won't reach the mother in time. I charge at the giant; he swings a meaty fist at me, and I duck quickly beneath it. But in an instant, a sharp pain stretches across the back of my skull like a lightning strike and I'm engulfed in darkness.

Good men wait while great men take control/
Civilians stay and kings take over the world/
Weak men watch while strong men tear down the walls/
Most men can't but a prince can conquer all.

"The Prince" by Ascending from Ashes

CHAPTER 1

By the time the news started reporting the attack on Brawnwyn Castle, I was already getting escorted into the car waiting for me out front. My trip to Lyndstel was being cut short. I was scheduled to meet with the Prime Minister in regards to economic hardships Lyndstel was currently experiencing, and how the Fenrir realm would be assisting in its reconstruction. According to my personal assistant, Zoe, it has been postponed indefinitely until the matters at Brawnwyn were handled. She told me all of this while power-walking beside me from my hotel suite to the car. I have a feeling Prime Minister Freige is going to be questioning the authenticity of this emergency. He has the bad habit of assuming any missed meeting is fueled by an ulterior motive, and then responding to it with passive aggression. That will be another headache for me to deal with.

Zoe also mentioned that she was doing her best to handle the media coverage on the attack. She said something about leaked footage and camera copters flying illegally over the castle to broadcast the damage. I nodded and agreed with the measures she deemed necessary to take. I was not in the mental state to suggest anything. My mind was focused on one thing.

One person. I need to call him as soon as I am in the car to make sure he is all right. I can hear him now; *Yes, I'm fine. I talked to the Staxeons and convinced them not to hurt anyone. They saw reason and apologized for everything.* That would be insane for most people, but with him it is entirely possible.

In the backseat of the black bullet-proof car is the head of the castle guard, Rhett. His short and muscular frame has ample leg room in the back of the spacious vehicle. His brows are knitted together and his mouth is in a thin, hard line surrounded by a neatly trimmed reddish-brown beard.

"What the hell happened, Rhett?" I ask as the door closes and the car begins to move.

"I am so sorry for this, Your Highness," he replies. "They managed to distract the guards at the gate with a burning tower. They then had another group infiltrate the castle from the sewers. This was a thoroughly planned attack, sir."

"What damage did they cause?"

His jaw clenches. "They caused very little damage to the property, sir."

I give him a puzzled expression. "Little damage? So what did they do? Did they take something?"

Rhett's face hardens even further. I didn't know that was possible. He lowers his eyes and then brings them to mine. "They took two things, sir. A Resident of the castle…and…"

I stare at him waiting to hear what it was, but he doesn't continue. He keeps his jaw clenched, his brows furrowed, and his mouth in a thin line. He is looking at me as though I will know what they took. I will know exactly what it was that was done to my castle. I have received this look multiple times, and it is usually accompanied by something I have done. Something that I knew was wrong yet did anyway. Those times I deserved the look, I do not think I deserve it this time. At least those times I knew what I had done to merit the look.

But this time I do not know. I do not know what they could have possibly taken that Rhett cannot even say to me. The crown? The jewels?

. . .

Oh…

My heart sinks into the pit of my stomach. "No," is all I manage to say.

"I don't know if they thought he was you or if they took him as ransom."

"No."

"We will get him back, sir."

My fists clench.

"Your Highness, we will get him back. We will find them both, and he will be returned to safety."

I am losing control. I can feel the heat rise from behind my neck. I swing my fist into the glass and shatter it. The car swerves and Rhett quickly orders the driver to keep going. He then leans toward me.

"Cal, we will bring him back."

I bring my eyes to Rhett. "Yes we will."

He sits back. "The guards managed to apprehend one of them. He is in custody now. I will question him and we will find Lorkan and bring him home."

I look out the shattered glass at the city blurring passed. I know we will find him. I know we will bring him home. I know this because if we do not, I will set fire to this entire realm.

CHAPTER 2

The criminal apprehended from last night's attack on Brawnwyn is shackled to a chair in the dungeon below the castle. He looks like a typical Staxeon with his partially shaven head and white twisting tattoo wrapped around his neck and shoulder. His nose looks broken and blood is dried on his lip and chin. I walked toward him and collide into Rhett's outstretched arm.

"You stay here."

"What?"

"You don't go near him."

My jaw clenches but Rhett does not move. He glances at a guard whom understands his unspoken order and moves in front of me. He then ignores my furious scowl and walks toward the prisoner. The Staxeon keeps his mouth in a firm line and does not look up at the towering mass of muscle in front of him.

"Where did the rest of your clan go?" Rhett asks sternly.

The Staxeon remains silent and does not lift his gaze. Rhett squats down to meet the criminal's gaze. "Where. Did. The rest. Of your clan. Go?"

"You'll never find them."

I clench my fists. I will slaughter this soldier in front of me and the seven in this room to break every bone in this son of a bitch's body. Rhett glances over his shoulder at me; the Staxeon lifts his eyes to mine.

"You will never see them alive. Not until you give us what is ours."

"And what exactly do you think is yours?" Rhett asks.

Something moves quickly across the Staxeon's face. His eyes flicker down and to the side, searching for the answer to that question. After a moment, he turns his scowling face to Rhett, then slowly brings his eyes back to me. "Your *prince* knows what is ours. Our say. Our rights!

Our rights!" He continues to scream the same two words at me as Rhett stands and motions to the guards to silence the criminal. The guards place a silencing plate over his mouth and the screams stop, but he continues to shout them with his angry eyes focused on me and his entire body trying to tear away from the chair he is secured to. Rhett walks over to me.

"That—that's it? That's all you're asking him?"

"He's not going to tell us where Lorkan is. They left him behind meaning he probably doesn't know enough to be of use to us. Or a threat to them."

I clench my fists. My heart is pounding and my skin is burning and I just might erupt. Rhett puts a hand on my shoulder and I have to look at his stern face. "We will find him."

"How? How!? How are we going to find him? We don't know where to fucking begin!" I bark.

"Our best hunters will be sent to find him." I pace, keeping my eyes fixed on the floor and my boots, because if I keep looking at Rhett or at the chair that held the prisoner, my skin will explode. "We will send them out in droves, Callum. They will scour this entire realm until they find him."

Rhett takes hold of my shoulders and keeps me still. He forces me to look at him. My skin is on fire and I can hear the glass of the cells around us tremble and crack. I'm losing control again, but a part of me doesn't care. If I lose control, I'm capable of destroying everything in this room. But at least then I will be free to find Lorkan and hurt whoever necessary to do so. But I would hurt Rhett in the process.

"We. Will. Find him."

I fight to breathe. I fight to focus. I fight to keep my strength under control. The trembling glass silences. I exhale.

"I want your best teams assembled to find him. Every inch of Fenrir needs to be searched. Every rock, every cave, every home. He needs to be found, Rhett. He *needs* to be found."

Rhett nods and drops his hands from my shoulders. "We'll be sent out in two hours, sir." With a soldier's nod, he turns and walks down the dungeon corridor; the orders he speaks into his ear piece fade before he disappears into the elevator. I turn my head to the empty chair; it crushes into itself and clangs loudly onto the floor.

"Sir, are you all right?" A guard jogs toward me, notices the crushed metal chair, and brings his confused look back to me.

"No, I'm not." The guard opens his mouth to say something, but I cut him off. "The prisoner, where is he?"

"He's being processed into his cell, Your Highness." I run to the processing area. "Sir, wait!"

"Leave me with him," I order the guards surrounding the prisoner. He still has the silencing plate over his mouth. His dark eyes glare at me furiously.

"Sir, it isn't safe—"

"Where is he?" I lift my hand to the Staxeon's face, and with the twist of my wrist, the silencing plate is ripped from his skin. He howls in pain and collapses to the floor.

"Sir!"

"Your Highness!"

The guards' voices are blurring into a dull annoyance of sound. I resist the urge to force them into unconsciousness. I kneel in front of the Staxeon, take hold of his jaw, and lift his face to mine.

"Where is he? Tell me where he is, and I will let you go." That is a promise I should not be making given that the High Court will not allow him to be set free. But I don't have time to care what the High Court will decide. I need answers to find Lorkan because I don't know how much time he has.

"Godless creature," he growls. "You will be punished for your godlessness. Staxos will protect me. I will be rewarded for my faith. My loyalty!"

I take hold of his throat and pull his face close to mine. "Your god will not protect you from me."

"You won't find him…" he croaks through my grip. "Until we take what is ours."

"*What* is yours? What do you *think* is yours?"

He tightens his lips into a thin line. I tighten my grip around his throat and his eyes widen.

"Cal, let him go."

Rhett.

The Staxeon brings his maddening eyes to Rhett standing behind me then back to my face. I release the prisoner's throat; he starts coughing and gasping for air. I stand and turn to Rhett. His eyes are darker than I have ever seen them before. He keeps his eyes focused on me as he speaks to the guards.

"Get the prisoner processed. Put him in his cell. And you," he points to me, "come with me." He turns and I follow him out of the unit. I take a last look over my shoulder at the prisoner. He smirks triumphantly at me just as the guards replace the metal plate over his mouth. I break his arm. They can't hear him scream.

Rhett and I walk in silence down the dungeon corridor. I look at the empty cells wondering which one the Staxeon will be thrown into. I notice the one occupied cell with its frosted glass. My stomach tightens and I force myself to keep following Rhett. That one cell holds the last Staxeon who managed to break into Brawnwyn almost five years ago. *Take what is ours*, he had said. The other Staxeon. They came to free him. And failed.

And took Lorkan instead.

Rhett and I step into the elevator. Once the doors close, Rhett finally speaks; "You are to stay away from him."

"He said they are going to take what is theirs."

"I'm aware of that, Callum. He said it to me, too. And that's not the first time I've heard it. Staxeons have been shouting that same message since I was a cadet in the Academy." He turns to me then with his jaw clenched. His hands are behind him in his usual soldier's stance, but the anger on his face is undeniable. "He told you nothing different. You learned nothing new. So what did you accomplish other than choking him? Do you feel better? Has that brought Lorkan back?"

"Stop talking to me like a toddler, Rhett."

"Stop acting like one," he growls. He turns back to face the elevator doors. "The Queen is arriving soon."

Rhett is out of the elevator a fraction of a second after the doors have opened. He leads the way to the troops assembling their equipment. They turn to me and salute before returning to their task at hand.

"I've assembled thirty teams of ten of our best hunters. Ten teams will be sent out by airship to the furthest reaches of the realm, ten travel on foot starting from Brawnwyn, and the remaining ten will travel by motor. I will be traveling with the team to Bastian City; it is the largest city and has the greatest number of hiding spots. Once a region is clear, we will radio back to the castle tower and mark it off. Zoe is arranging for you to declare a State of Emergency and make the people aware of what is about to happen."

"What of the Staxeon region? The area beyond Namor Forest?"

"A team is heading there as well."

"I want to go with them."

"You already know my answer to that," Rhett replies without looking at me.

I open my mouth to say something that will most likely get me the worst death glare from Rhett I have ever seen, but I snap my mouth closed as an idea pops into my mind. I don't argue. I nod instead.

"We will be moving within the hour," Rhett adds. He disappears through the crowd of soldiers. I turn and bump into Zoe. She looks up at me from behind her silver glasses.

"The media is ready for your announcement, sir. The prompter is ready. Follow me." She goes over what I will be saying as we walk to the media room of the castle. I try my best to concentrate on what Zoe is telling me, but it's difficult with my brain spinning out in multiple directions. Thoughts of Lorkan being held by the Staxeons makes my blood run cold; my growing plan to get him back bubbles to the surface, but I have to push it down again until I can execute it. Right now I have to issue the State of Emergency and keep the people of Fenrir calm. Even while I'm boiling with rage.

CHAPTER 3

"Cal! I'm so glad you're safe!"

My mother's flight landed while I was giving the State of Emergency address, so she had to wait in her office until I was finished and Zoe told me where to find her. As soon as I walked into her modest office, she leapt to her feet and threw her arms around my neck. The last time she hugged me this tightly was four years ago when I told her I had fallen in love.

She holds my face in her hands and examines it, as if I'm hiding a wound somewhere and she is determined to find it. "I'm so sorry about Lorkan."

I can't hold it in. Tears pour out of my face in a violent wave and I just drop my head into her neck. She hugs me tightly and kisses my head. She has always had this power over me. No matter how hard I fight to keep my emotions under wrap, they come pouring out of my eyes once she asks me if I'm okay or if there is something wrong. It's an unstoppable force.

"Oh sweetheart," she whispers. "He'll be okay. They will get him back. He'll be fine. He's strong."

"He was alone," I whimper pathetically. "He was alone."

That is the idea that kills me the most. I wasn't here with him. I couldn't fight for him. I couldn't fight and kill to protect him. If I had been here, I would have slaughtered every Staxeon that dared to touch him. They wouldn't have even attempted to enter this castle if I had been here. He would be standing beside me right now, rubbing my back and keeping me calm. He would be the voice of reason, reminding me that everything is still intact and we will rescue the kidnapped Resident. On top of that, he would know the Resident's name and his entire life story by heart.

"He knows you'll come for him," she tells me as she kisses my head again. "He knows you love him, and that you will move Heaven and

Earth to get to him. He knows." She wipes the tears from my face, even though more are taking their place.

"I love him. I can't lose him, Mom. I can't."

"You won't. You won't lose him, Callum, you won't." Now she's crying. Now we are both sobbing. "They will find him and bring him home." She sniffles. "Rhett showed me the teams he has assembled, and they will not sleep until Lorkan is back home. He is a prince of Fenrir as much as you are, and they will bring him home."

On cue there is a heavy knock on the office door. We wipe our faces of their tears, and Mom opens the door.

"Your Majesty, the troops are all set to deploy at your say," Rhett tells her. I look at him and he turns his body to face both of us.

"Deploy them," she answers. "Be careful."

"Yes, Your Majesty." He gives both of us his usual soldier's nod, and walks out of the office. I dry my face and walk to the open office door.

"I want to see them off."

My silver-haired mother nods and cradles my face again. We walk out side by side and she gently rubs my back; her hand drops when we reach the front courtyard. Almost all of Brawnwyn is gathered to watch the troops deploy. Rhett is speaking into his ear piece as three hundred equipped soldiers board ten airships, ten bulletproof motor trucks, and fifty speed cycles. The airships leave first, lifting swiftly into the sky and traveling in ten different directions. The motor trucks take off next, traveling in a single file down the main entrance-to and exit-from the castle. Rhett mounts his speed cycle – the only one with a single seat – and leads the way out of Brawnwyn. I feel my mom's hand squeeze my arm as we watch the line of soldiers shrink into the distance.

I hate standing here watching them leave. Watching them go after Lorkan. I should be doing that. I am the one most capable of finding him and bringing him home safely. I'm the one with the power to slaughter anyone in my way to make sure he is safe. I should be out there looking for him. I should be hunting down the Staxeons that took him. And I will be doing just that.

"I'm going to find out how they got inside," I tell my mother. She nods and gives me a gentle smile. Fighting back the tears that threaten to spill from my eyes, I walk through the crowd of Residents, listening to them mutter greetings and Your Highnesses as I pass. I do my best to smile and be courteous as I move through them, but I can't be my "most presentable" self, as Zoe refers to it.

Then I feel a small, cold hand on my face and I stop. I turn toward the child that touched me, and she has big blue eyes stained red; she must have been crying.

"I'm so sorry, Your Highness. Don't do that, Greta." The woman holding the child pulls the girl's hand down to her side.

"That's all right."

"He saved me," the girl says.

I freeze and look at her. "What?"

"He saved me. He tried to save my mommy, but they took him."

"Lorkan? You saw Lorkan?"

She nods and tears start to stream down her face. "He saved me from the mean men. They were taking me and mommy." She cries harder, and the woman soothes her and combs her fingers through the girl's dark hair.

"Her mother was taken?"

The woman nods. "Yes, Your Highness. The guards were able to save Greta, but couldn't get to Kaia. She says Lorkan saved her."

The little girl, Greta, turns her tear-stained face to me. "He's – *hicc* – my hero."

"Mine too. Those soldiers out there are looking for your mother right now, and they will bring her back. Her and Lorkan." A small smile touches Greta's face. I bring my eyes to the woman holding the girl. "Thank you for taking care of her."

"We all are," she replies, turning her body to motion to the other Residents on either side of her. I smile weakly and nod before continuing on to the security tower.

Brawnwyn is an expansive property with the castle sitting at its center. It was built during my great-grandfather's reign over a century ago. He wanted it to be a safe haven for all citizens of Fenrir whom did not have their own homes. The ground floor's entire east wing is Resident living quarters, providing almost four hundred civilians with a home. The west wing is divided into a public school for children ages five through eighteen, and a training institute for those eighteen and older. Only three rooms within the castle are strictly for my family's use: my parents' bedroom, my bedroom, and my mother's office. The sub-ground level holds our dungeon, the guards' quarters, the armory, and the stronghold; the top floor is the library, media room, and kitchen and dining halls.

Lorkan has been a Resident of this castle since he was an infant, yet we had not officially met until I was seventeen and he was eighteen. We didn't even meet during school which we attended together; my parents didn't want me segregated from the people of Fenrir. Instead we met while Lorkan was working in the armory. I stumbled upon him taking inventory and proceeded to pester him with questions to prove he was supposed to be there. We became friends quickly.

Behind the castle is the courtyard and garden where I would usually find Lorkan sitting on the bench beside the stone statue of my father, staring up at the sky with a faint smile on his lips; that's always his favorite place. In the center of the courtyard stands the main security tower; it's the tallest of the three towers. The other two towers are beyond the courtyard, situated against the gate surrounding the edge of the property. The tower closest to the entrance of Namor Forest is where the guards were distracted by the burning pile of twigs. And I will deal with those easily fooled morons later.

The elevator doors open and I walk into the main security room. The guards and officers all stand and salute; they say "Your Highness" in unison like a chorus. One officer that looks vaguely familiar to me walks over and extends her hand.

"Sir, I'm Officer Gilbert. Agent Ryckoff put me in charge of the castle security while he's on the search."

The petite brunette gives a firm handshake and does the same curt, soldier nod that Rhett always does. It takes me longer than a fraction of a second to remind myself that Agent Ryckoff *is* Rhett; I've forgotten he even *has* a last name.

"Nice to meet you, Officer Gilbert. Can you run me through the logistics of the search?"

"Of course, sir." She spins on her heel and leads me down the aisle between desks and computers toward a giant screen at the front of the room. It's a map of Fenrir with blue dots clustered at Brawnwyn Castle, spreading in different directions.

"The blue dots, as I'm sure you've guessed, indicate the carriers traveling across Fenrir. Each one of us is in direct communication with every team, all thirty." Gilbert points to her earpiece; "I'm linked directly to Agent Ryckoff. He's also receiving a constant feed of this map, knowing where every team is as well."

"Have you looked into how the Staxeons made it into the castle in the first place?" I ask.

She nods. "Yes, sir." She walks over to a short, round metal projector. She presses a button and a projection of Brawnwyn Castle illuminates in a silver-blue light. She turns the projection around and zooms in on the basement floor. "Right through here, sir," she says as she points to a sewer grate opening. "They managed to cut through the steel pretty cleanly. We don't know what tool they might have used, but it's more high-tech than I thought the Staxeons were capable of."

"That is something to be concerned about."

"Agent Ryckoff said the same," she replies.

"Has this…exposure been covered?"

"Engineers have already been in and out and repaired the damage. They're also looking into how to strengthen the structures to prevent this in the future, but that will take time."

"And make sure every other potential entryway is reinforced. I do not want this happening again anytime soon."

"Already done, sir."

"Officer Gilbert, Agent Taine has just reported back. Eloine has been searched and cleared," a seated guard announces.

"Mark it on the map," she replies.

"Already done, ma'am."

Gilbert and I look at the oversized screen displaying Fenrir; the small village of Eloine receives a little green flag. Gilbert brings her eyes back to me. "Anything else I can provide for you, sir?"

"No, not—yes, actually. Can I get one of those ear pieces? I want to know every update with the search as soon as they happen."

"Yes, sir." She double-taps her ear piece. "Roy, can I get another ear piece for the Prince? Set it to receive every update in the search. Bring it to the Prince as soon as possible. Thanks. It will be up and running in a minute, sir."

"Thank you."

"You know that they work under water and one hundred feet below ground. Just be careful around electrical equipment. All of these tech advances, but we're still fighting with electrical disturbances," Gilbert explains with a chuckle.

"Maylor has been cleared by Agent Slattenko," a guard announces. "And has been marked on the map." Another green flag pops up on the screen. A tall guy with an IT badge on his chest walks in carrying a small grey box.

"Your ear piece, Your Highness." He opens the small box. I take the ear piece and slide it into place.

"Can you hear me?" Gilbert asks; her voice echoes into my ear and in front of me.

I nod. "Loud and clear."

"You're linked in to Officer Gilbert and Agent Ryckoff," the tall IT guy says.

"Thank you. Both." I nod. Gilbert salutes me; the IT guy notices this and awkwardly salutes me as well. I walk out of the room to a muttering of "Your Highness" and "sir" from the seated guards in the room. The small village of Lare Hollow was cleared before I reached the elevator; Rhett announces into my ear that his team is entering Bastian City.

That gives me more than enough time.

CHAPTER 4

Judging by how long we've been walking, I would say we are at least two miles from Brawnwyn. But that's not counting how much time I've lost when I was unconscious, so we could have covered who knows how much ground in total. We could be ten miles from Brawnwyn, and I wouldn't know. I also have no idea what direction we're going in. I know we have made three rights, two lefts, one right, two lefts, and a right. While I can remember every twist and turn, I have never had much of a sense of direction to keep a proper idea of where we're going. We could be nearing Rutterford which is about an hour's walk from the castle, or we could be just outside of Oléar Park which is a three hour air ride.

Basically, I know nothing.

Not true. I know a few things: 1) The shackles clasped to my wrists and ankles are made of a metal I didn't know Staxeons were in possession of. The Staxeon clan is a small group that have been known to cluster deep within Namor Forest due to its lack of human inhabitants and distance from most civilizations. Where they got these metal shackles is a mystery. Probably the same place they got the guard grade pistol they tried to shoot me with. From the armory within the castle? But that requires security code access. So I don't know much about that actually, but it's something to think about.

2) There are eight Staxeons we're walking with, including the giant one who dragged out the female Resident walking beside me. None of them have spoken to us, but they occasionally whisper to one another. One particularly odd thing occurred about three-quarters of a mile back when our group was nine Staxeons. One of the white-tattooed men just stopped walking with us. He just stood there as we carried on, and when I looked back to see where he was going, he walked into a wall and vanished. I am assuming there was a door somewhere that I couldn't see, but either way, he just deviated. They said nothing about

him deviating, it just happened without a word. It was a premeditated action. But why? And where was he going?

3) These tunnels we're walking through were not made by any government departments of Fenrir. These are custom built tunnels made evident by their crude structure and the dim lights placed several feet apart from each other. The tunnels are narrow, but made to accommodate the large size of the giant, so he was in mind when they were built. Which gives me the distinct impression that Staxeons built these tunnels, and that would require either an extensive period of time or a far greater number of Staxeons than I know exist. And built these tunnels specifically to harbor this giant and to travel underground without being seen. And to make their way into Brawnwyn Castle and kidnap Residents and bring them to God knows where.

Residents and me. But I was an accident.

"Stop," a Staxeon with a deep scar across his cheek announces. He slides the leather bag off of his back and pulls out the box of rolls. The giant guides the woman and me against the wall of the tunnel; we sit down obediently. Scarface hands us one roll each. The Staxeons walk several feet away from us, sit in a circle, and start feasting on large sandwiches and pass around leather thermoses. I turn to the brunette woman beside me. She's nibbling quietly on the roll, staring off into nowhere.

"Are you all right?" I ask her.

She slowly turns her face to me. She has a narrow face, a pointed nose, and bright green eyes. "Fine, thank you," she whispers. She takes another miniscule bite of her roll. She's not paying attention to eating.

"You're worried about your daughter."

Worry contorts her face and her lips begin to tremble. "I don't know where she is. Or if she's okay." Tears run down her face. I can't wrap my arms around her with my wrists shackled together. I lean closer to her instead.

"She's okay, I'm sure of it. The guards got to her before we were taken."

She turns her tear-stained face to me. "Thank you for saving her. Thank you so much. I-I owe you…everything."

I shake my head. "You owe me nothing. I'm sorry I couldn't get us out of this."

"I'm just glad they didn't get her. She's more important."

"Why were they after you?" I ask.

She blinks several times and her mouth opens, but she just shrugs. "I don't know. Ransom, maybe?"

"Maybe," I reply. That isn't true. It's not a maybe as to whether or not she was a ransom; she wasn't. That would not make any sense at all. If you're going to demand a ransom from Queen Thestera or Prince Callum, you take someone who matters most to them. It would make more sense to kidnap me or Rhett even. But a Resident of the castle and her daughter? That is not the way to go about demanding a ransom.

So either she honestly has no idea as to why she was taken, or she knows but won't tell me.

"I'm Lorkan, by the way."

"Kaia," she answers.

"How long were we walking before I woke up?" I ask.

She slowly shakes her head and her eyes stare at her feet. "It feels like we've been walking forever. Without seeing outside…I don't know how long. Two hours? Two days?" Her voice trembles with the last two words and more tears spill from her eyes.

"It's going to be okay. We *will* get out of this. I know it. I know all of Fenrir is out looking for us right now."

She brings her red-stained eyes to mine. "How can you know that?"

"Because I know Prince Callum. And he won't rest until he finds us. I promise."

What I don't mention is that he is probably going to do something incredibly stupid to find us.

To find me.

CHAPTER 5

A little more than five years ago, the Staxeons launched an attack on Brawnwyn Castle. It was a group of about fifteen or twenty of them. They charged one of the side entrances with the fewer number of guards. They were brandishing old-world weaponry: rifles and long swords. They caused very little damage. It didn't take long before they were outnumbered by our guards, and once they caught a glimpse of me approaching, they retreated into Namor Forest. All but one escaped. The High Court found him guilty of attacking Brawnwyn Castle, attempted assault on the Queen and Prince of Fenrir, and assault against the guards of the castle. He was sentenced to thirty years imprisonment. That one Staxeon has been sitting in a cell in the dungeon below the castle since that day.

The Staxeons haven't attacked in five years. Not to retrieve their fallen comrade, not to destroy Brawnwyn, not to take a ransom. Yet now they have. They have suddenly decided this one Staxeon was worth coming back for. But why? Why take so long? Why hold out for all those years? And why enter from the sewer grate below the castle but crawl out to the main level to encounter a Resident and Lorkan?

It makes less and less sense the further down the elevator descends. By the time the doors open, the idea that the Staxeons attacked to free this prisoner seems unlikely. Staxeons are not exactly brilliant, but they aren't stupid enough to bypass their purpose, risk getting caught, and ruin their entire mission.

Unless their mission was to take Lorkan.

The cell occupied by the first captured Staxeon is in the middle of the dungeon's corridor. Every occupied cell is locked with a unique key code, and the glass is frosted so the prisoner cannot see out and no one can see in. This glass is also unbreakable, sound proof, and contains a life monitor to make sure the occupant is still alive. That last part only matters because if I murder this creature, the entire dungeon will know of it and guards will come running.

I write the five character code into the blue digital screen on the side of the frosted glass with my fingertip. Once the glass has gone from opaque to transparent, my eyes lower to the Staxeon seated on the floor with his back against the glass. He has a book in his hand and his arm is propped on his knee. He doesn't stir, he merely tilts his head ever so slightly in acknowledgement of my presence.

"How can I help you, Your Highness?" He turns the page slowly, but doesn't look at me. His voice is deep and smooth, and there is a musicality to it as though he knows something I don't.

I peer down each end of the corridor; the guard on duty must be making his or her rounds. I don't know how much time I have.

"Last night a group of Staxeons attacked the castle and kidnapped two people. I need your help to return those people to safety."

He scoffs. "Why would I help you do that?"

"Because they entered the castle and did not bother to rescue you."

"I don't mind that all that much. It's quite comfortable here." He tilts his head to read the other page of the book. "I have a bed, three square meals, books: what more could I ask for?"

I clench my jaw and curl my fingers into my fist. "Your freedom."

He lowers the book and looks at me over his shoulder. His icy blue eyes narrow and the corner of his mouth curls slightly upward. "My freedom? I reiterate my previous statement regarding my more than comfortable living conditions."

I force the growing fire within my throat to subside, but it isn't listening to me. I'm not listening to me. The glass begins to the rattle. I tighten my fists, focusing my power, and send the book from the prisoner's hand. It slams against the wall and drops to the floor. He merely arches an eyebrow at me in response.

"Someone's losing their temper."

"Tell me where your people have taken him."

"Him? I thought you said *two* people were taken last night? I suppose only *one* truly matters to you."

I inhale deeply and exhale. "Tell me where the Staxeons would take *them*."

He stands slowly and sighs. He's taller than I expected, a few inches taller than I. He doesn't look like the typical Staxeon, but that is most likely because of his time here. His silver-grey hair has grown out from its partially-shaven style, but his white tattoos are still visible from under the collar of the white prisoner's uniform. He slides his hands into his pockets as though we are friends having a chat after a long absence.

"Why would I know the answer to that?" he asks with the tilt of his head.

"Because you are a Staxeon and you know how your people think."

"I haven't been around *my people* for almost five years. What could I possibly know about them? I don't know how they work or where they're bringing your precious boy."

I slam my hand against the glass. His body is lifted into the air and his eyes widen in shock. His small bed slams against the wall.

"Be careful, Prince," he warns. "You kill me, you will never find him."

I slam his body down to the floor of the cell. His bed falls back into its proper place, barely missing his hand. He sits up and arches another silver eyebrow at me.

"You really should keep that under control, Your Highness."

"Tell me where he—where *they* are."

He's silent for too long of a moment. His blue eyes stare into mine as he slowly gets to his feet. He approaches the glass.

"I can't tell you where they are, *but*… I can show you."

"Show me?"

"I can track them."

"Track them?" Is he serious? I should kill him for wasting my time.

"They tend to move around a lot. Staxeons – last I was with them – didn't like to stay in one place for long. That's the main reason why your hunters probably won't find them."

"Niles and Drakaan have both been cleared," Officer Gilbert tells Rhett in my ear. I wait to hear Rhett tell me to stop talking to the prisoner and leave the dungeon. I wait to hear him yell at me for doing something so stupid. No matter where he is, I always have a feeling Rhett knows exactly what I'm up to.

But he doesn't say a thing. He doesn't reply to Gilbert, he doesn't tell me to stop acting like a child, his end is silent. He doesn't just appear behind me with a firm hand on my shoulder to tear me away. It's just me and the Staxeon standing and staring at each other in silence.

"Your Highness?"

And the guard making her rounds through the dungeon. I turn to face her, but instead I'm met by Zoe. She gives me a puzzled look behind her silver glasses and walks over to me. As she approaches, she realizes the cell's glass is clear and stops moving. Her eyes move from the prisoner to me.

"What are you doing?" she asks.

I swipe the cell glass to its opaque state. I turn to Zoe and try to think of a lie, but nothing is coming to mind fast enough. Only the truth keeps popping into my mind. "Trying to find Lorkan," I answer. It is the truth, just not all of it.

She nods and accepts the response. "Be careful," she says as she crosses her turtleneck-clad arms over her torso. "Staxeons can't be trusted. Besides, Rhett and three hundred of Fenrir's finest are searching for Lorkan. They'll find him."

No, *I* will find him. I will find him with the help of a captured Staxeon locked away in the cell right next to me. I will be releasing this Staxeon so he can lead me to his people and so I can slaughter them and bring Lorkan home. I can't say that to Zoe though; she'll turn on me. I need her to leave. But how do I send her away without it being completely obvious as to what I'm doing?

"Are there still reporters outside?" I ask.

She shakes her head quickly and pushes a loose strand of dark hair behind her ear. "No, sir, they're all gone. I was looking for you to let you know the castle is cleared of them. You'll be giving another address tomorrow afternoon with an update on the search."

I hope by then I'll have Lorkan home, and I can update the search by ending it. I nod. "Thanks, Zoe."

"Of course, sir. You should get out of this dungeon and try to get some rest." She gives me a small smile before turning and walking to the elevator. Once the elevator doors close, I turn back to the cell and re-enter the key code. The glass clears and the prisoner is standing exactly where I left him: staring straight at me with his hands back in his pockets.

"Once we find them, you are going back to this cell," I tell the silver-haired Staxeon.

He pulls his mouth into a thin line and tilts his head. "Mmm, I don't think so." He shakes his head. "No, that won't be the case at all. Once we find them, I'm free to go."

"No, absolutely not, no."

"Then consider your boy lost."

I punch the glass and it simply vibrates in response. The Staxeon hardly flinched. Instead he grins to reveal an array of teeth.

"What happened to you not needing your freedom? What happened to enjoying your living conditions?" I growl.

He shrugs. "Changed my mind. Especially after realizing how much you need me."

"Once we find Lorkan…*and* the Resident, and bring them back to Brawnwyn safely, I will pardon you. But *only* when they are *both* brought to the castle *alive*." He nods. "And should you turn on me at any point, I will destroy you. I will not hesitate." His smirk widens and he nods again.

"Understood. So will we be leaving under the cover of night?"

"No," I snap. "As soon as possible. I'll be back." Without another word I frost the glass and walk back to the elevator.

CHAPTER 6

The doors to my bedroom are partially open. I peer inside before pushing the doors open. The room is empty. The bed is made. A dark grey crown sits on the floor. I walk slowly toward it. My eyes start to burn with fresh tears. I slide onto the floor and sit in front of the crown.

He was probably wearing it when the Staxeons attacked. Or at least trying to wear it. This crown is too small for Lorkan. He always tries to wear it, but it just sits on the top of his head like a tiara. I smile at the image of him putting my crown on his head and balancing it.

Why is it so heavy? He's asked me. Then he would try to keep his head up and his neck straight, but it would weigh on him quickly. He'd groan and laugh before placing it back on the pedestal where it usually sits. *It looks better on you anyway,* he said on multiple occasions. I never agreed with him though. Everything looks better on Lorkan.

"Candeleron has been cleared."

I place the crown back on its pedestal before walking to my closet. I don't spend much time in my closet, I usually wear the same combination of four items on a daily basis: black T-shirt (for informal days) or black or white button-down (for formal days), black slacks, black leather jacket (for informal days) or black blazer (for formal days), and my black and silver boots. For extremely formal occasions, I have to actually go into my closet for my tuxedo or decorated royal uniform. On the rarest occasion, an occasion that has never occurred before, I have my battle uniform.

It stands at the back of my walk-in closet in its own wardrobe. I pull the two wooden doors open to reveal the black body suit on one dress form and the dark grey armor set on the other. A "C" with two crossed swords behind it is lightly carved into the chest plate. The helm, which is more a decorative feature than an actual protective piece, is dark grey with gold trim lining the face and a silver wing that rises from the front and curves slightly backward. Leaning in the corner of the wardrobe behind both dress forms is a sword and a hilt without a blade. The ceremonial sword is a saber with a black, silver, and gold hilt; *Royal Family of Fenrir* is engraved in the blade.

The battle sword is far more unique and most people don't even know of its existence. When my mother had first given me the bladeless hilt, I stared at it in confusion for several long minutes. The hilt was heavy and made of the same material as my crown. As I opened my mouth to ask my mom what it was in my hand, the blade slowly emerged from the hilt. It wasn't the usual steel like the ceremonial sword or like the swords our soldiers carried. The blade was black, and the way it bent and moved gave the illusion of a viscous texture, but it solidified into something stronger than steel.

It was then that I finally recognized the weapon. The last time I had seen it was when I was about twelve or thirteen, and it was a mere glimpse during the greatest and bloodiest battle Fenrir has ever seen. My father wielded it against the foreign invaders and defeated them. It was the only weapon powerful enough to stop them. He explained to me that two men brought it to him when the invaders arrived. He never used it after that battle, and I never saw it again. I thought it was buried with my father until Mom brought it to me.

You control it, she told me. *You control the blade. It will grow as long, as wide, and in the shape you want it to take. It can be whatever you need it to be. Your dad said it was meant for you.*

I never had a reason to take any of these items out from their place in the wardrobe. Battles were not a common occurrence in Fenrir. Even the assault on Brawnwyn by Staxeons – including the cretin waiting for me in his cell – did not result in any casualties. It was not required of me to brandish a weapon of any kind, let alone the most powerful blade in the realm. Wars among nations – other than the occasional Staxeon attempt at a coup d'etat – were unheard of during my father's reign, and even during most of my grandfather's. That long-lasting peace across the realm was the main reason why we were so unprepared when the invaders attacked. This blade was capable of stopping the Exitians, it is more than capable of handling whatever the Staxeons throw at me.

I put on each layer and slide the hilt into the holster at my hip. It takes some adjustment for me to get comfortable in the stiff armor. I walk out of the room with one last glance at my crown.

CHAPTER 7

"Your Highness," the guard on duty gives me a puzzled look at my armor as he salutes me.

"What is your name?" I ask him.

"Officer Den, sir."

"Officer Den, I am going to order you to do something that you will *not* want to do. But remember it is an order and you have to obey it." Den's face gets even more confused. "I am taking out the prisoner from that cell, and you are taking his place."

"What?"

"I know it does not make sense, and I will explain when I come back. But until then, I need you to trust me and obey this order. You are taking his place, officer, and you are not reporting it." I walk to the cell and write in the key code.

"Sir, I—I can't let you do this," Officer Den manages to croak. He brings a trembling hand to his holstered pistol. The cell glass clears and the Staxeon inside is sitting on the floor with his skull hanging between his knees and his hands on the back of his neck. He lifts his head to look at me with a hint of surprise on his face; he wasn't really expecting me to come back.

I look over at Officer Den whom has pulled his pistol from the holster, but isn't aiming it at me yet. "Sir…"

"Officer Den, you are disobeying a direct order from your prince. I am ordering you to holster your pistol and stay in this cell."

He shakes his head slowly. "Sir, I can't let you do that."

I didn't want to do this. I lift my fingers and pull the pistol from his hands. With the curling of my fingers into my palm, I squeeze on Officer Den's throat until he blacks out. His body slinks to the floor. I make sure he's breathing clearly before opening the cell. The prisoner steps out slowly, and I place Officer Den's body on the bed carefully.

The life monitor in the cell skips only a beat before resuming. I take Den's ear piece before locking the cell and frosting the glass.

"You will go to any lengths for him, won't you?" the prisoner says with a smirk. I stop myself from punching him.

"I will. And I will kill you in an instant if that will promise me Lorkan. My purpose is to find him and the Resident...Kaia," I'm proud of myself for remembering her name. "Once they are back at Brawnwyn, you will be pardoned. But *only* when they are *both* back here safely. Until then, I do not trust you. You are a blood hound I need to find them. Should you turn on me, I will destroy you. Should you prove to be of no assistance to me, I will throw you back in this cell. Do you understand?"

"Yes, sir," he replies with that same obnoxious smirk. He looks down at his white prisoner's uniform. "You're not expecting me to go out saving your people in this, are you?"

"Follow me." I lead the way to the guards' quarters within the dungeon. It is an expansive room filled with rows of lockers where the guards keep their personal affects. I open a locker and hand him the guard's uniform.

"So tell me what you know," he says as he pulls off his shirt. The white tattoos wrap around his entire torso in sharp lines and edges. "Who was taken?"

"Lorkan and a Resident by the name of Kaia. From how I understand it," from how Greta explained it to me between sobs, "Lorkan and Kaia were taken last night from near the front of the castle. She was with her daughter when the Staxeons came in."

"Did they get her daughter?" he asks as he pushes his head through the neck hole of the black undershirt.

"No, Lorkan got her to the guards," I reply.

He nods as he pulls on the armored pants. "Any idea why they were taken?"

"Royal Pointe has been cleared."

"I was hoping you would have an answer to that one."

He tilts his head side to side as if tossing ideas around before shrugging. "Not sure. Any idea if they were trying to take Lorkan, then the woman and her daughter got in the way?"

"Other way around, from how her daughter explained it."

The prisoner stops struggling with the armored vest and looks at me. "Her daughter? You spoke with the girl?"

I nod. "Yes. She told me that Lorkan saved her. That he tried to save her mother, but then he was taken." My heart aches again, but I can't cry in front of the prisoner. Lorkan is exactly the type to rush in and save people. Even if the odds are against him. He would sacrifice his own life for the lives of people he has never even met before. That's just how he is.

I love that about him.

I also hate it.

"Hmm, it sounds like they were trying to take the woman and her daughter." His head is echoing within the locker as he searches for something. "Are they of importance to you? Are there shoes in here?"

"Check the next locker." I wave my hand and pull the locker open.

"Ah, yes!" He grabs the boots and sits on the bench to put them on. "So, the Resident and her daughter: any importance?"

I shake my head. "Not beyond being a Resident of the castle."

"Mount Vaston is clear."

He does that head tilting again while looking down at the boots. I don't know if he is questioning why the Staxeons were after the woman and her daughter, or if he likes the boots he's wearing. "Well, hopefully if we find them, it won't matter why they were taken." He hops to his feet and smiles. "So much better than that prison napkin your men had me wearing. So do I get a weapon or do you not trust me enough for that?"

I scowl at him and hand him Officer Den's pistol. "Do not make me regret this."

He smirks again; "I'll try, Your Highness."

"So where do we start the search for them?" I ask.

He examines the pistol as he answers; "We start with their last known location. Which was…?"

"Somewhere beyond Namor Forest."

His eyebrows raise. "Wow, really? Haven't moved since then? Talk about lack of progress." He shrugs again and shoves the pistol into the holster. "That makes things easier for us. Lead the way, Your Highness."

I walk through the dungeon and out the back security entrance we use when escorting high priority guests and prisoners. I keep the prisoner beside me rather than behind me as we walk. I know fighting whatever Staxeons we come across won't be the most difficult part. Getting through this without punching *this* Staxeon in the face, however? *That* will be the biggest trial.

LEAKED FOOTAGE OF PRINCE CALLUM FREEING STAXEON PRISONER

Click the link to watch the SHOCKING footage!

CHAPTER 8

We are down to five now Five Staxeons and Kaia and me. I've noticed where the Staxeons disappear to; there are other tunnels buried in different directions. I can't see far enough down the tunnels they are slipping into to see where they are going, but that is where they are going. That doesn't help me much in the scheme of things, but it keeps me wondering where they're going and why we are dwindling down to a smaller group. What happens at the end? Will they all split up into different directions? Or will we finally arrive at a destination?

"Does it feel like we're going around in circles?" Kaia asks me quietly.

"I have no idea where we're going. But we've been walking for how long now? When do we stop?" I reply.

"We stop when we say you stop," the lead Staxeon growls over his shoulder at us.

I wonder how many more of the group will leave us. Will it come down to the lead Staxeon and the giant? Will it come down to only the giant? Because if that is the case, I think Kaia and I could take him down. Long enough at least to disappear down a tunnel and make a run for it. But we have no idea where we are or how to get out of these tunnels. We've been walking for hours, days maybe, for miles, and we've made turns and twists. We would be able to retrace our steps, but only until when I awoke; I don't know where that would leave us. Without food or water, we probably wouldn't make it. At least not that far.

But what other options do we have?

"Where are we going? We've been walking for hours," I say loud enough for the lead Staxeon to hear me. He stops and turns to face me. He's shorter than me, but stocky with that deep scar across his cheek; it stretches from his ear to the corner of his mouth. His eyes are a dark brown, almost black, and they stare into my eyes as though they can see through me. It is an uncomfortable feeling having him look up at me like this.

"You are lucky you're still alive, boy," he hisses at me. "Keep quiet or that will change."

Someone else would have gotten nervous. Someone else would have been afraid of his threat and been silenced by it. But I know he won't kill me. If he does, that unleashes a full-fledged war against the Staxeons. And Prince Callum will obliterate each and every one of them. So I can't stop the smirk that creeps onto my face.

"Lucky? You need me alive or else all of Fenrir will destroy you," I retort.

Kaia looks nervous in my peripheral vision. I keep my stance firm and my shoulders square. I'm not afraid of this cretin, even with my wrists and ankles shackled. I know they won't kill me, so there's no reason for him to threaten that they will.

"Godless creature," Scarface mutters under his breath.

"I'm not godless," I snap. I tower over the Staxeon; I can probably knock him unconscious with my limbs bound. The three others and the giant watch us closely, waiting to pounce. "I believe in God. The true God. The God that encourages peace between all living things. Not destruction like the one you worship."

Scarface scowls —or maybe it is his attempt at grinning— as he speaks. "Our God is the *only* God. And He will punish your kind. He will—"

"He won't be doing anything. Other than take us in circles."

The giant growls loudly and moves toward me with a heavy-thudded step. Kaia gasps; I plant my feet and brace myself for the hit. Scarface lifts his hand and the giant reluctantly stays still; he growls in frustration at the unspoken order.

"There's no sense in your false bravery, boy," Scarface says. "We may not kill you without invoking the wrath of your prince, but we can kill *her*," he points to Kaia. Her green eyes widen at the scarred hand in her face. "And only hurt *you* in doing so."

My jaw clenches and my heart sinks. Staxeons may be foolish enough to take me, but they weren't that foolish in taking her. If it wasn't for the giant, I would incapacitate Scarface and the others long enough to get us out of here. But that is not an option. And now, talking back and standing up to them is not an option either. Not when they are threatening to kill Kaia. I will not be responsible for leaving Greta motherless.

I step back and keep silent. Scarface grins again knowing he has won. "Now move." He turns and leads the way down the dimly lit tunnel. Kaia keeps her eyes nervously fixed on me. I start moving and she follows; the giant drags his massive feet behind us; the three others walk beside us. Kaia moves closer to me.

"I won't let them hurt you," I whisper.

"I don't care what they do to me," she says quietly. "As long as they don't get my daughter."

CHAPTER 9

The search through Bastian City is going smoothly. Most of the residents have been completely cooperative. They had their doors open before we even arrived, welcoming the soldiers in to search every nook and cranny for our missing Residents. Two agents and I were clearing the Mayor's home, Bastian Manor, when Officer Gilbert tried to mask her panic with a false calm voice.

"Agent Ryckoff, I'm sending you something I think you need to see."

I never like the sound of that. I don't like anything someone *thinks* I need to see. It's usually something I don't *want* to see. Something that will ignite fury through my skin and make my jaw clench to the point of cracking molars. Something that will most likely result in me smashing something within arm's reach.

"What exactly is it I need to see, Officer Gilbert?" I ask as calmly as I can fathom. Is it a ransom from the Staxeons? Are they finally demanding something in return for Lorkan and the Resident?

"It's...footage, sir," she manages to reply. "I don't know how it was leaked to the press, but it's all over the Internet."

I clench my jaw and close my eyes. For. Fuck's. Sake. I hate the Internet. I hate it. I hate people who leak footage onto the Internet. I hate people who leak footage to the press. I hate press who hide in trees and bushes and in sewer grates to get pictures and video of Cal and Thestera. I hate Staxeons. Right now, I hate pretty much everyone.

"It's sent, sir," she adds.

I glance over my shoulder to make sure I am alone in the hallway of the mayor's home. A young woman dressed in a manor uniform walks by me and gives me a pleasant nod. I don't want to see whatever it is Gilbert just sent me with people around. Especially innocent people that may see me blow up. I make my way down the hall and step into an alcove.

I pull out my mobile and tap on the new file received. The footage unfolds into a holographic projection in front of me. The headline hits me first, then my eyes widen at the actual footage: Prince Callum releasing a Staxeon prisoner from his cell and leaving the dungeon.

I can't believe it didn't occur to me that the thing I would *need* to see was the ultimate stupidity only Callum is capable of.

I'm going to kill that kid.

"Agent Ryckoff, sir?" Officer Gilbert asks me after my long bout of silence. I look down at my mobile which is now cracked and dented in my palm. I knew I'd smash something.

I sigh and growl. "Get that footage off of the Internet. Speak with Zoe, I'm sure she's already on it, but make sure she gets that handled. Any idea where the Prince and the prisoner went?"

"They left through the hidden passage behind the dungeon, sir."

"Of course they did. Everyone is to continue the search," I tell her. "Finding the Resident hostages is still top priority."

"Are you going to speak to the Prince?" she asks.

"I doubt he will answer my phone calls."

"I mean through the ear piece."

"He has an ear piece?"

"Yes, sir, he requested one before he left. I didn't know he was leaving, but he said he wanted to be kept up to date with the progress of the search."

He's been listening. He knows where we've searched, where we've cleared, and he knew I was in Bastian City where it would take at least two hours to get back to the castle. By that time, he could be anywhere depending on what mode of transportation they've taken. He planned this rather thoroughly except for the part of being seen on the security visuals.

How did the press even get those security visuals? They got it from someone in the castle. Now we have another issue. I growl again.

"I'll speak with him. Thank you, Gilbert."

"Yes, sir."

I release an exasperated sigh. I rub my forehead as a dull throbbing pain starts to pulsate from the base of my head to between my eyes. Only this kid makes my head do this. But right now, I need to think. I need to think clearly because he isn't. Although, really, when does he ever?

He's using the Staxeon to find Lorkan. He's been in that dungeon cell for almost five years, so he will only help him as best as he remembers of the Staxeon clan. They aren't going back to their village beyond Namor Forest because that has already been cleared. So where are they going?

The footage of them leaving was from within the castle. It was the security visuals only accessible by the security guards, agents, Zoe, Thestera, Cal, and me. Someone in the castle leaked that footage, but why? So the Staxeons know that Cal has left the castle? So the people of Fenrir will think Cal is working with a Staxeon prisoner? All of the above perhaps.

I tap my ear piece. "Cal. Cal, you need to answer me. Footage of you and the prisoner leaving Brawnwyn has leaked onto the Internet. Whatever it is you are doing, stop it now."

There's no response.

"Return to the castle now, put the prisoner back in the cell, and speak with Zoe. Deliver some address to the people of Fenrir. Deem it a hoax, explain it's a misunderstanding. Do something to stop the uprising that could be triggered by this."

Silence.

"Damn it, Callum. Answer me. You could be risking Lorkan's life right now with what you're doing. You are risking his life, your life, and your entire reign over Fenrir."

I sigh at the silence. I rub my scalp, trying to massage the burning annoyance out of my head. It isn't working.

"Don't get killed," I say finally. Too many memories of death and pain flood my mind, and I have to force it back before I slip into a catatonic coma. "Don't get killed. Don't kill a bunch of people. Do not let your power get out of hand, Callum. And *don't* get seen by any other cameras or people."

I sigh again. He isn't going to answer me. But I didn't expect him to. He's being far too stubborn and hard-headed for me to get through to him right now. But I don't need to get through to him. What's more important is finding Lorkan and the Resident. I have to continue on with the mission, that's what a soldier does, and that was my promise to Cal.

"Sir?" Agent Crest says nervously from behind me. I sigh as I turn to face him; whatever it is he's about to tell me is just going to be another stress for the shit pile I am already buried under. I freeze.

Agent Crest has his hands in the air with a pistol aimed at his head by an oversized Staxeon. Agent D' Lorne is standing in a similar position. Behind them is a flood of Staxeons – at least twenty of them – staring at me with menacing smirks, aimed pistols, and gleaming blades.

All I can do is release another annoyed sigh.

Fuck.

CHAPTER 10

Namor Forest is the largest forest in Fenrir, which is why the sun was setting behind the trees and engulfing us in a slow darkness by the time Officer Gilbert's voice said that the Staxeon outpost had been cleared. Lorkan and Kaia are not there. And now I am in the middle of the dense forest with Reinhardt – whose name I learned when I told him to shut up about "we should have taken a speed cycle" – with no plan as to where to look next. The plan I was relying on has just failed me. If Lorkan isn't at the Staxeon camp beyond Namor, where is he? Where did they take him? Where are they hiding him? And why haven't they requested a ransom or made demands yet? Why did they take him if they were just going to hide him from me?

"The Staxeon camp has been searched and cleared," I say aloud. Reinhardt is walking a few feet ahead of me when he stops and looks at me. His eyebrows are knitted together and his jaw clenches; he actually looks angry.

"How well did they look?" he asks.

"Well enough to know Lorkan and Kaia are not there. Fuck," I growl. "Now what? Where would they have gone?"

Reinhardt is silent. He turns his silver-haired head slowly, looking through the darkening forest. He then brings his face back to mine. "I want to search for myself. They missed something." He resumes walking through the forest. I run to him and grab his shoulder.

"The hunters will be coming back through the forest to continue their search. They cannot see us. They definitely cannot see *you*." I point to our left. "We will move that way. Go around them."

"We're losing time," he growls as he starts moving in the direction I have pointed to.

Night has fallen by the time we step out into the clearing beyond the forest, and I have not answered Rhett's pleading message. I couldn't say a word. If I replied, said anything, even cleared my throat, he wouldn't have stopped until I came back. He would not give up. He almost convinced me with his speech, but I knew – I know – I cannot stop the search for Lorkan. No matter what.

I have never seen the Staxeon camp with my own eyes before. I only had the images Rhett would put in my head with his vague descriptions, and it was never simple getting answers from Rhett about his past before he was Head of Security in Brawnwyn. This was not how I imagined it.

The camp is spread over a large clearing, but there are only a handful of cloth and fur tents scattered around. The only light through the darkness comes from small fires still burning between every two tents. A crudely made rack of weapons stands against one tent; an oversized wooden wagon sits empty several yards from the nearest tent; the largest tent is farthest away and covered with a dark cloth; a wooden pedestal with nothing on it stands in the center of the camp. This is where Lorkan's captors live? This is where the biggest aggravation against Fenrir and its people reside? In small cloth tents with one rack of weapons?

"This…is not what I was expecting."

"Nor I," Reinhardt replies. I look over at him and can make out a faint look of confusion, and maybe even concern, on his face. "It didn't look like this when I was last here."

"A lot has changed in five years," I reply.

"Hmph," is the only answer he provides. He starts walking toward the tents and I follow closely. I keep my hand over my hilt tapping against my hip.

Reinhardt stops abruptly before we have reached the nearest fire and two tents. I follow his gaze to the ground and spot something shining in the firelight. He kneels and picks up the item, lifting it between us.

"Is that…a metal bracket?"

"Yes, it is." Reinhardt moves it between his fingers in the light. "But where did it come from? Or what did it fall off of?"

"That…that looks like a piece from an auto pistol the guards carry. Maybe it fell from one of their weapons." I do not see the importance of this item. What does it matter if there is a random piece of scrap metal on the ground? Or if it is a piece of metal that fell from a guard's weapon? How does this help us find Lorkan?

Reinhardt shakes his head slowly. "No, this wouldn't have just fallen off. This is a big piece. Even *your* guards would have noticed. This is from something else."

"What?"

"That, Your Highness, is the question."

I roll my eyes as I walk toward the nearest fire. I have a feeling he is doing that annoying smirk, and if I see him do it, I'll hit him. I hate trying to see anything in this darkness. The moon isn't even out tonight, so all we have are the small fires throughout the camp. And my mobile phone, which I have almost forgotten I even have. I pull the thin item from my pocket. Ignoring the six missed calls from my mother, and eleven missed calls from numbers I don't recognize, I tap the flashlight application to life. The white light illuminates the ground in a broad beam.

I make my way around one of the tents and peer inside. I can make out only a dark unmoving form inside, and even with my flashlight, I have no idea what it is I'm looking at. I lift my eyes to Reinhardt moving behind the tent to speak, but the air is knocked out of me by a heavy force colliding into my stomach, and then again when my back hits the hard ground.

I grab my assailant by the throat and throw his body off of mine. I get to my feet quickly. He is crouching low to the ground, preparing his next attack. He growls angrily. In the darkness, I would have guessed it was an animal of some kind. But the flickering fire proves it is a human with a partially shaven head and the familiar white swirling tattoo wrapped around his arms and neck. His eyes move from me to Reinhardt.

"Goran?" Reinhardt asks. Of course he would know the one that attacks me. And of course he would start a conversation with him rather than fighting him. Staxeons never change; what did I expect?

The Staxeon – Goran – bounces his eyes between Reinhardt and me. He finally pushes off the ground and charges for Reinhardt. I am taken by surprise at this reaction; however, the greater surprise comes when Reinhardt balls a fist that glows white and blue and collides it into Goran's face. His body drops to the ground and he is still.

"He never did like me," Reinhardt says nonchalantly. He stretches out his fingers and his hand returns to its normal color. I point to his hand.

"What was that?"

The annoying smirk returns to his face. "You're not the only one in this realm stronger than most."

He kneels beside Goran, and with a grunt, Goran is on top of Reinhardt with his hands around his throat. I rush toward them, but Reinhardt has already curled his silver-white glowing fist and cracked it into Goran's jaw. The man rolls off of him again and groans in pain. The silver-haired Staxeon places his hands on Goran's ankles; blue-white ice spreads from his skin onto Goran's and anchors him into the ground. He struggles and growls, which I now believe is a Staxeon habit.

"Whoa, whoa, easy there," Reinhardt says to him as he holds his wrists down, covering them in ice.

I wonder how long he's been able to do that. And I wonder why he never tried doing that to get out of his prison cell. Or maybe he did and it just didn't work. We've never tested the cells against ice before.

It's not exactly something we expect to be a form of attack from within or outside the cell.

"Your fellow lunatics, where have they gone?"

Goran scowls angrily. "You honestly think I will tell you anything? You took my daughter from her family. You corrupted her. Turned her into a heathen like you. Burn in Hell."

That last statement was hissed through gritted teeth. I am almost surprised by the level of hatred this man seems to have for Reinhardt. But I would hate him too if he took my daughter and did who knows what to her. I didn't think Staxeons turned on each other like this, but it's not that surprising. Even within their clan they can't seem to get along.

But right now none of that matters. They have Lorkan and will do just about anything to him if I don't reach him in time. It has already been an entire day, and I have no idea if Lorkan is hurt, alone, fighting to survive, or…

No.

I know he's alive. I know it in my heart. I just have to find him. And this interrogation is taking too long.

I step toward Goran; "You may not tell him anything, but you *will* tell me." I lift my hand and curl my power around his throat.

"As you can see, Goran, our prince does not like you withholding information from him."

"I will die before speaking." he manages to spit out.

"You're a stubborn fool as always," Reinhardt hisses. He looks up and his brows furrow as he scans the open field. "Where is everyone?"

The man remains silent; I squeeze a bit harder on Goran's throat. He gasps and pulls his mouth into a tight, defiant line. His eyes look feral. He's truly willing to die to keep from telling us where Lorkan is.

Reinhardt stands and begins to walk toward me. He stops abruptly and his face contorts into a puzzled expression. I release Goran whom starts coughing and breathing heavily, and follow Reinhardt's gaze. There's nothing to look at; just other tents and fires several yards away and the empty pedestal. I'm starting to lose my patience.

"What? What are you staring at?"

"That tent..." he says vaguely. I may just punch him on principle, but I do need him to explain what it is he's talking about. "It's the General's tent and usually sits in the center of the gathering. It shouldn't be there."

"What does *that* matter?" I bark.

He growls but does not say a word before sprinting toward the dark tent on the edge of the field. This tent is larger than the others by a significant measure. The fabric is lush and deep red; I can't help but touch it to make sure it's as luxurious as it appears. I can hardly fathom where the Staxeons even managed to obtain this high-end fabric. I'm so busy questioning the origins of this item to even notice Reinhardt has already dipped inside the tent.

With a hand on my hilt, I carefully push the drape to the side. The darkness has engulfed Reinhardt and I can't see even a hint of his silver head. I look over my shoulder where the struggling Staxeon lies. He is fighting angrily against his icy constraints to no avail. My mobile is on the ground somewhere near him after he tackled me. Which I did not adequately punish him for.

"Reinhardt?"

The female voice catches my attention immediately. I bring my eyes back to the darkness within the tent. A clatter of voices erupts, all speaking over each other in panicked whispers. Female, male, and all varying in youthfulness. How many people are in there? It sounds as though there are at least ten of them, most likely more. This tent doesn't appear large enough from the outside to fit that many people comfortably inside.

A part of me wants to step further inside the tent to see where these voices are coming from, but I don't allow myself to move. This could all be an elaborate trap. I still can't trust Reinhardt or the Staxeons. And if it is a trap, I'll slaughter everyone in my way. Anyone who tries to attack me will be destroyed, and I will tear Reinhardt apart limb from limb just for wasting my time. He's keeping me from Lorkan, and that crime is punishable by torturous death. My thoughts are quickly silenced when the tent is illuminated in an orange glow with the crackle of a flame. Now I *have* to look inside.

"Tannah? What-what is this?"

I step into the large tent. Reinhardt is several feet ahead, squatting and staring down at the ground. There are oversized wooden tables on either side of the tent, and stacks of empty weapon racks in three haphazard piles; a vintage flame lantern is on the ground. Reinhardt had mentioned this was the General's tent, but it looks more like a storage tent full of garbage. I have to remind myself that this is a Staxeon camp, not Brawnwyn or Fort Helm. Their General's quarters are obviously very different from the ones I've seen. Although I'm amazed Staxeons ever had a General whom required his own tent.

"Reinhardt, you have to get us out of here," the female voice – Tannah, I presume— says. I stand beside Reinhardt and look down toward the voices. Large steel planks appear to be imbedded into the ground, stretching about twelve feet across. The spaces between planks are no more than two inches wide. Numerous pairs of eyes are staring up at me with panic behind them. How many people are inside of this small, metal box?

As though I took a pistol shot to the knee, I drop to the ground and peer through the slits. "Lorkan?! Lorkan!" He's here. We found him. Reinhardt actually managed to find him. And those foolish hunters cleared this area but didn't find Lorkan here. I make a mental note to permanently release each and every one of them from their positions.

"Lorkan?" the voices begin to question.

"No, Your Highness, he isn't here," the female voice says.

My heart clenches and feels as though it is going to stop beating. I think I might prefer if it did. The voices all blur together into a dull buzzing of sound. Lorkan is still out there somewhere. He is still lost, still taken, and I still have to find him.

"Get down and cover your heads. I'm going to try to shatter it," Reinhardt's voice pierces through the blanket of sounds. I look over at him as his hand begins to glow silver-white again. A blaze of anger erupts from the base of my neck and washes over my scalp. I extend my hand and curl my fingers into my palm. Everyone inside the small cell shrieks as the metal slabs are ripped from the ground and crushed into a ball. The compacted metal clangs to the ground behind me as I walk out of the tent.

I run both of my hands through my hair, threatening to tear out every strand. Another dead end. Another useless derailment from finding Lorkan. Did Reinhardt plan this? Bring me here to release his people from their cage? Who put them in there anyway? It doesn't matter. All that matters is that Lorkan is not here and my search continues for him. But where the hell do I search next?

A warm hand touches my upper arm and I move instinctively. The elderly woman jumps and the elderly man beside her takes hold of her shoulders. I relax slightly at the sight of the small people standing before me. The woman has pale eyes surrounded by deep set wrinkles, and a thin layer of white hair on top of her head. The man beside her has no hair at all, and the white tattoo is faded across the folds of his cheek.

"We are so sorry Lorkan was taken, Your Highness," the woman says softly. "He appears to be such a lovely boy."

I blink rapidly and clench my jaw as I nod. "He is," I manage to croak with a curt nod. The woman's hand presses against my chest, right over my heart. She looks into my eyes and smiles softly, like a grandmother would do to her grandson.

"Staxos will protect him."

The force of my power can break her frail hand, wrist, arm, and kill her with ease. A part of me is extremely tempted to do just that. To destroy this entire camp and everyone in it. But I control myself. Instead, her hand is pushed away from me by an invisible presence. Her light eyes search mine; I easily recognize the fear behind them.

"Your ridiculous religion is the reason he was taken from me. Your Staxos protects *nothing*. Only *destroys*."

She staggers backward as I walk away from them. A whimper reaches my ears and the man asks her if she is all right. I'm out of ear shot to her response. I can feel the power radiating off of my skin with pulsing heat. I struggle to control my breathing and what I *want* to do to this entire place. If I follow through with that desire, this field will be nothing but a lifeless crater where the Staxeons *once* lived.

"Cal!"

I stop but don't turn to look at Reinhardt. I wait for his outrage at how I treated the woman. For storming away. For using my power against her. I curl my fists, ready to punch him as soon as he asks me what I was thinking. I'll find Lorkan on my own. I don't need his help or the help of any Staxeon to find Lorkan. And it will feel amazing to make someone hurt as much as I do.

"They don't know where they took Lorkan. They've been trapped in that cell for weeks," he says instead. "Probably months."

I want to punch him anyway, but—miraculously – I don't. I turn to face him slowly as he turns to look at the people. This would be the ideal time to bury my fist into his skull. I don't know if I would stop once I started. My knuckles would be broken and bloody, and

Reinhardt's bones would be a sticky paste against my skin before I ceased.

"Grey Victoria has been cleared."

"What are they doing?" Reinhardt asks aloud. He jogs briskly toward the people newly freed from their cage standing around something. I look over at Namor Forest. I could leave. I could return to Brawnwyn and wait for Rhett and the others to find Lorkan. I can go home, apologize to Mom for sneaking out and freeing a prisoner in the process—which will merit a jail sentence from the High Court.

That is what awaits me if I go home now: a jail sentence, an empty bed, and the verbal chastisement of the century. Not sure if that last one will come from my mother or Rhett.

Releasing a painful sigh, I walk toward the crowd of Staxeons. As I approach them, I can hear their murmurs and voices grow louder. The silver-haired man is standing on the outside of the group, asking what the commotion is and what it is they're so concerned about.

"It's gone," I hear a man whisper. "It's gone…"

"What is gone?" I ask. A young man about my height turns to me with glassy, red eyes.

"Staxos. The statue of Staxos…it's gone."

"When did this happen?" Reinhardt asks. I notice his blue eyes are wide, staring at the empty pedestal before him incredulously. His mouth is partially open and he's not blinking. I look around at the others; some are crying, most have their hands over their mouths in disbelief. The elderly woman from before has her eyes closed and her hands folded over her chest; her lips are moving silently.

"What is this?" I ask Reinhardt. Several others look at me in horror, some in sadness.

"This is the pedestal where the statue of our god, Staxos, is supposed to be," a fox-faced girl answers. Her voice sounds vaguely familiar. She is working to project a hardened exterior: her expression is stern and her jaw is tight. But her arms are wrapped around her torso as if without them she may collapse into pieces.

I cannot say I've ever seen a group of people react so strongly to an inanimate object before. Certainly not a statue.

Reinhardt kneels beside the wooden pedestal and runs his hand over the top, examining the wood closely. A message is carved into the side of the wood:

Our God Staxos
His power is to be revered
His mercy is to be respected
In time His presence will return to our world,
And He shall cleanse its sins to restore righteousness.

"Who would do this?" someone's voice cracks.

"We *know* who did this," Fox-Face snaps.

"True Staxeons would *never* take Him down. So why is He missing?"

"And where did they put Him?"

I can see what Reinhardt's fingers are outlining: a faint discoloration in the wood creating almost a perfect circle in the center of the pedestal. I assume that is where the statue belongs. He plants his palm in the center and it glows; white ice cracks and pops as it spreads across the wood and encases the entire object. The pedestal becomes a glassy structure, reflecting the bodies surrounding it into blurry, dark forms.

"Reinhardt, what are you doing?" Fox-Face barks. The others around us continue to whisper and hiss at one another. I can make out a few questions similar to the one just shouted at Reinhardt. Good to know the list of people whom cannot stand him continues to grow.

"They moved Him for a reason," he replies without even looking up at the woman tugging him away from the pedestal. He curls his fingers into a fist and knocks his knuckles against the frozen structure. It shatters, and the pieces fall straight down a deep hole. My eyes widen at the dark well. The people around me gasp, followed by a slew of louder questions and murmurs.

"What the hell?" someone breathes.

Reinhardt looks up at me and waves his hand; "After you, Your Highness."

CHAPTER 11

When I first joined the Fenrir military, I was assigned to the Staxeon Task Force. Priority was to always keep an accurate and up to date count of the Staxeon population. They were a powerful nation of people advocating for religious equality and acknowledgement in the realm's political sphere. They often did not want to discuss their believed injustices in forums within "hostile territory," as they referred to it. Instead, political figures would take the journey to Staxeon lands. My group was responsible for assuring those meetings remained peaceful at all times. That was a calmer time with far less extreme Staxeons. And of course that was all before the foreign invasion which was a bit of a distraction. But before that time, Staxeons maxed out at about fifty to sixty people. Given the number of Staxeons currently holding Bastian City hostage, I would venture to guess their numbers have increased significantly. There are at least twenty of them ushering us into the Great Room of Bastian Manor. So there must be another twenty or so keeping the citizens scared and contained. And according to Officer Gilbert, other teams in other cities have not reported back. They're probably dealing with similar situations. If forty Staxeons are at each of those locations, that puts their numbers at around one hundred sixty.

That is one hell of a growth.

Our survival depends on how well they have planned this siege. Currently, they have planned it well enough. They have overrun the city and have managed to round up my team and the city guards. They took our weapons –not without struggle which almost led to the deaths of two of my agents – and are now ordering us to remove our armor. The shackles are coming in, and I know once those are put on, escaping this will be considerably more difficult.

All of the choices made by the Staxeons have been logical ones, but they have made too many mistakes.

First, they have put all of us together: my team and the city guards, which puts our numbers at almost twenty. Twenty of us, twenty-four of them in this room with us. Every one of my team is trained to fight at least two people at once, which puts my team's number at twenty and ten city guards totaling out at thirty. We outnumber them.

Second, only some of the Staxeons are using our auto pistols and putting on our armor. The ones who are seem to be a bit uncomfortable wearing the gear and are visibly examining our weapons with fresh eyes. They won't be able to wear the armor well enough to stop our attack, and they will not handle our weapons to their advantage. Not to mention we know where the weaknesses are, and we know how to exploit them.

Third, we still have our ear pieces. I can hear Officer Gilbert report that teams in Fort Helm, Oceanside, South Goldwell, and Bastian City have not reported into headquarters. She knows something is wrong and is handling it accordingly.

"Should team leaders be listening but unable to speak: may the dreams of our children become realities."

That line is a famous quote from King Caderyn's last speech before he passed. It is now used as a code for Fenrir military to do what is necessary until cavalry reaches them. Right now we are hoping that cavalry is on its way, but there's no way to know when they will arrive. So until then, it is up to us.

But that's all we need.

Because the fourth and biggest mistake the Staxeons have made: we are still alive.

A tall Staxeon stands in front of me; I have to look up at him to make eye contact. He's holding one of our auto pistols to my chest and glaring at me.

"Remove your armor," he growls. I glance around me at the team all moving slowly and watching me intently. "Now!" The Staxeon barks. I bring my eyes back to him.

"May the dreams of our children become realities," I say calmly.

Before the Staxeon's eyebrows can knit together in confusion, I grab the auto pistol, smash it into his nose, and shoot the closest Staxeon. As I move my aim across the room, the rest of my team attacks our captors. Gunfire erupts through the room, echoing off of the marble floors and pillars. A Staxeon slams down on my weapon, and I break his nose with my forehead. I dart behind another pillar where an aiming Staxeon is standing. I slam my boot into the back of his knee and crack the butt of my weapon into his face.

"Incoming!" an officer shouts as more Staxeons start to flood the doors of the Great Room. I empty the first clip of the auto pistol into the onslaught of Staxeons. I snatch a sword off of a dead Staxeon and charge toward the others. I bury the blade into an enemy's rib cage as my left elbow smashes into the temple of another.

"Get down!"

I don't look for the voice, I just drop down to the floor. A barrage of shots goes over my head like a blanket of gunfire. A limp body falls on top of me, and I feel the blood drip onto my cheek. Once silence falls and one of my men gives the all-clear, the dead Staxeon is pulled off of me.

"Agent Ryckoff, are you all right?"

I look up at Officer Till; she extends a hand and helps me to my feet. "I'm fine. Any casualties?" I ask loudly as I examine the room of lifeless and bloody bodies.

"Three down, sir," one officer answers. "Two from the city, one of ours. And Agent D'Lorne has been hit."

"Get him medical attention immediately." I tap my ear piece with one hand and wipe the blood from my cheek with the other. "Gilbert,

Ryckoff. We don't need the cavalry. Bastian City will be cleared momentarily."

"Agent Ryckoff, sir," Gilbert releases a sigh of relief. "Happy to hear your voice. We'll redirect reinforcements to Fort Helm. What's happening, sir?"

"Phillips, Slater, pick eight others to go with you and sweep the rest of the mansion. Move quietly, stay on alert, aim to kill any Staxeon you come across." I return to my ear piece. "Staxeons ambushed our team, and from what you mentioned about the other teams not reporting in, it would seem as though other major cities are being overtaken as well. This is organized, planned, but my guess is that there is a bigger attack in the works. Most likely on Brawnwyn. Lock down the castle, put the Residents in the stronghold, and secure the queen in the Guard Tower."

"Yes, sir."

"We will be returning to Brawnwyn as soon as possible."

"Yes, sir. Be careful, sir."

I lead the way out of the Mayor's Mansion to clear the rest of the city. There are only another handful of Staxeons we need to dispose of.

Fifth mistake.

CHAPTER 12

"This is unbelievable," I said once I landed on my feet from the fall down the hole hidden underneath the moved Staxos statue. This tunnel is large, dimly lit, and was not made by Fenrir government workers. "How? How did they do this?"

Reinhardt dusts himself off and examines the walls. "This was not done when I was here, so I would guess they have been working on this for five years."

"This was not done with our knowledge either," Fox-Face announces as she peers through the hole in the ground. Her eyes are wide and she shakes her head slowly. "We had no idea…" her voice trails off.

"But how? The tools required for a tunnel this size…where would they even get them?" I ask.

"I don't know. I wouldn't doubt it has something to do with that metal piece found above. But right now, how they built these tunnels doesn't matter. Let's hope they lead us to Kaia and Lorkan. Tannah," Reinhardt says as he tilts his head back to look up at the people above ground. The fox-faced woman is still staring down in disbelief at the hole. Her eyes slowly move to Reinhardt and she is able to focus. "Keep them safe, and keep Goran restrained."

"Oh that won't be a problem," she retorts. "Be careful." She brings her eyes to me; "And good luck."

"What did you do to that man's daughter?" My question breaks through the silence as we jog down the tunnel.

Reinhardt's jaw clenches and he almost looks annoyed with me for asking this question. "I didn't do anything," he answers flatly. I remain silent, glancing at him repeatedly before he finally sighs and continues. "She made her own decision, and she chose me."

"Tannah? Is that her? Is that why he had her locked in that cage with the others?"

"No," he replies with the shake of his head. "Tannah is Goran's niece. But that has nothing to do with why they went crazier than usual and locked them into that cage."

"You do not have the highest respect for your own people."

He grunts. "How can you tell?"

"'Your fellow lunatics?' That man – Goran – called you a heathen. Seems as though you do not follow their way all that much."

"I don't respect any civilization that demonizes knowledge and free-will. Or holds their own people captive because they disagree with them."

"You believe that is why those people were in that cage? They disagreed with what the others were doing?"

"According to Tannah, that's how it started. Goran and the others started to get more extremist, more radical – even more than when I was there. When some started to stand up to them, actively disagree with their plans and claims, suddenly they were being thrown into that cage."

"They disagreed with taking Lorkan? Was *that* planned?"

"If it was planned, Tannah and those in that cage were certainly not a part of it. They most likely would have tried to stop them. So they had to be silenced. Irrational zealots."

"Irrational zealots? Are you not religious?" The idea is insane. He's a Staxeon. That's what their entire lives are founded on. They believe in their god Staxos, they follow their scriptures and beliefs, and they have slaughtered thousands of people in protection of those beliefs.

"I am," he answers. "I believe in a just God that does not smite people for questioning Him. There are radicals of every civilization, and *those* Staxeons – people like Goran – are the radicals of this one."

"To them, *you* are the radical."

He arches an eyebrow and grunts again as we follow the turn of the tunnel. "To them, someone who is born with a useful gift is a god.

Someone who chooses how to *use* that gift differently than how *they* deem suitable is considered a heathen."

I nod slowly. "You wanted to be captured."

"What?"

"You allowed yourself to be captured when your clan attacked Brawnwyn those years ago. It was the easiest way for you to escape them. Am I wrong?"

He looks at me as though he is about to refute everything I'm saying. He even opens his mouth to deny it. But instead he just sighs and turns his face forward. "Safer than returning to them having failed to kill Queen Thestera and Prince Callum."

We stop once we come to a split in the tunnel. We look both ways. "Shit," I mutter. "Shit! Which way do we go?"

Reinhardt looks both ways with a stern face. "We can split up. Go both ways."

I shake my head. "No, absolutely not. I am not letting you go on your own."

"You *still* don't trust me?"

"All of Fenrir does not trust you. I am not going to let you run off to find your brethren and turn on me. We are finding Lorkan and Kaia together. *You* will lead me to them. So pick a direction. You know your 'fellow lunatics' better than I do. Which way did they go?"

He growls angrily as he turns his head from side to side, looking down the identical tunnels. He glances back the way we came. "That way," he points to my left.

The dirt tunnel seems endless as we jog down its winding path. I am losing patience with every step we take. There is no guarantee we are traveling in the right direction, and if we are, it's taking far too long to find an end to this tunnel.

"I don't have time for this," I growl angrily. I lift both of us with my power and we glide down the tunnel faster than our feet could carry us. I've never done that before, and the headache building above my eye is my punishment.

"You couldn't have done this through Namor?" I hear Reinhardt mumble.

"Shut up," I snap. "Look!" We stop abruptly and drop to our feet; it takes Reinhardt a few seconds to steady himself.

There's one turn off that is only a few feet in length with a set of dirt steps leading to a door several feet up. I climb the steps cautiously and lift the crudely made door to peer into our destination. The darkness is heavy and I can't make out a single object or figure. I managed to forget my cell phone back in the Staxeon camp. I duck my head down to Reinhardt; "Hand me one of those lanterns."

I push the door open further and lift the lantern with me. The bulb illuminates a small area of this room, but there isn't much to see in it. We are in a large, cement cavern. It's empty, cold, and oddly familiar. I open the door completely and step out of the dirt tunnel onto the cement floor. I lift the light to see other parts of the vast room.

"What is this? A dungeon?" Reinhardt asks standing beside me.

I shake my head. "No. I've been here before," I reply. I walk to the right, knowing in my gut that is where I'm supposed to go to find a door. Nothing is on the walls, nothing is on the floor, and there are darkened lamps and lanterns on either side of the wide room. There is something in the far corner forming an odd square shape; cots and bed frames stacked and piled high.

"This is a strong hold," I answer finally. I turn my head and see the door in the corner. It's a heavy, steel door with bolts and barricades built into it. "We are in Fort Helm," I say aloud as the realization seeps in.

My ear piece suddenly shrieks into my ear and fills with static and white noise. I almost tear it out of my ear at the surprising blare of noise. The volume of the cacophony diminishes, but it remains a steady crackling with faint voices cutting in and out. Something must have disrupted the receiver while we were walking through the tunnel. I vaguely remember Officer Gilbert mentioning something about sound disruption when going underground. This is where Lorkan's memory would come in handy.

"Fort Helm? What the hell are Staxeons digging a tunnel here for?" Reinhardt asks me as I'm still shaking my ear piece.

I wonder that very question as I carefully push the door open. The screams and gunfire hit me before the light of the room does. I don't hesitate. I do not move quietly and cautiously. I do not peer into the room to assess the situation.

I take hold of my bladeless hilt and charge into the room. I hear Reinhardt bark something behind me, but I don't bother to stop and listen. Whatever protests he's shouting, he can keep shouting them. I'm going to find Lorkan.

The room we've entered is the secondary armory of Fort Helm. A handful of guards are attempting to barricade the entrance to the armory while three others are assembling their auto pistols and taking aim. One of the guards spots me and blurts out, "Your Highness?"

"Move!" I order. All but one dive away from the door; he gets slammed into the wall by the horde of Staxeons charging into the room brandishing pistols and curved blades.

They were not expecting me and their faces betray it.

Swords are raised and pistols are aimed at me. Before the first shot can even be fired, I pull my sword in front of me as it widens into a four-foot shield. Ammunition does not ricochet off of my weapon; the black, viscous substance absorbs them instead. I swing the blade, shattering the pistols and breaking some of their swords. In a fluid motion my elbow connects with the jaw of one Staxeon followed by my boot slamming into the back of another's knee. Blasts of gunfire discharge from the guards' weapons. Bodies drop around me as I push forward, making my way out of the armory toward the other Staxeons.

I slice through them, cutting down two more before the first body has fallen. Every part of me is a weapon: my fists crack into jaws; my feet burrow into stomachs; my elbows break arms. My sword takes any and every form I require it to: a six foot blade to impale several men at once; a bladed whip to reach the auto pistols aimed at me; a shield to deflect every shot sent my way. I am faster, stronger, and better trained than the Staxeons, but they are not harmless.

One wraps an arm around my throat and tugs me backward. Others charge for me, swinging swords and trying to take hold of my fighting limbs. An invisible force bursts from my body sending Staxeons scattering in every direction.

"Kaia and Lorkan!" Reinhardt shouts at me. His fists are covered in thick, white ice as he fights his own people. Ice breaks off in dusty shards with every hit he lands. "Where would they be held?!"

We came from the second armory, which makes it most likely that they would be kept in either the first armory or the prison. But that idea is quickly shattered as one of Rhett's agents runs toward me bleeding from his lip and panting heavily.

"Your Highness, Lorkan and the Resident are not here. We searched before the Staxeons attacked," he says.

"I'm searching again," Reinhardt retorts angrily. He runs through the raging battle of guards toward the prison. I run after him, using my power to throw Staxeons out of my way and knock them off of their feet. I push myself faster to go beside him.

"The prison's that way," I point to the right. "I'll search the armory." I turn left and run to the large steel building. My sword glides through limbs and torsos with ease. I do not pause to fight. I need to find Lorkan.

The first armory is larger than the second and guards are trying their best to keep the Staxeons out of it. I slice through the ones attacking the doors, and push my way through. I ignore the shouting of confused words and questions thrown at me, and run down the long corridor, searching through barracks and rooms for Lorkan.

"Sir! Sir!" A guard yells from behind me.

"Where are they? Have you seen Lorkan? Was he here? The hostages the Staxeons took from Brawnwyn Castle, were they here?" I ask as I keep running and throwing doors open.

"No, they aren't here, sir. It's been cleared out," the guard says as he struggles to keep up with me. "Sir, we have another problem! Sir"

I finally stop and look at him. "What?" I bark.

He fights to catch his breath as he answers me. "The Defender, sir. They took it. They had it reprogrammed and they took it."

My heart sinks. This cannot be happening. There's no way they reprogrammed it. How? How could they have reprogrammed something so high-tech?

"What? How? How!"

"They had pistols to our heads, sir," he blurts out. "They were holding our engineers' families hostage, threatening to kill them all if the machine wasn't reprogrammed."

"Reprogrammed how? To be operable by anyone?"

"To be operable by a particular blood sample. I don't know what kind."

A particular blood sample? What blood sample? What the fuck does that even mean? I'll figure that out later. I'll answer all of those questions once this uprising is over.

"When did they take it? How long ago did they leave?" I ask quickly. I start running to the exit of the armory. Lorkan and Kaia are not here. They will be wherever they are taking the Defender, and I have a pretty good idea of where that is.

"About fifteen, twenty minutes ago, sir."

"The prison is clear! They aren't here!" Reinhardt shouts as we meet in the center of Fort Helm. A Staxeon charges at me and I cut through him.

"They reprogrammed a machine being held here and took it. I think they're going to use it against Brawnwyn."

"What machine?"

"The Defender. It was built to fight off another foreign invasion after those Exitians attacked and nearly wiped out this entire realm. The people of Fenrir needed something more powerful than auto-pistols and air ships to fight those creatures off, so The Defender was commissioned. It was only completed a couple of years ago."

"They reprogrammed it? To do what?"

"It was built to only be controlled by me, but apparently they reprogrammed it to be controlled by someone else. I don't know who. 'A particular blood sample' is what the guard said. Which means nothing to me."

Reinhardt's face of fury falls immediately. His knitted brows separate and soften; his mouth loosens from its scowl and opens slightly; his height even appears to diminish. He looks straight at me, or perhaps even through me, and his skin pales. I plunge my sword into the stomach of another Staxeon, but I keep my eyes on Reinhardt.

"What? What? Reinhardt! Reinhardt, say something!"

He's unmoving. He's catatonic. His eyes finally move and focus on mine. "We need to get to Brawnwyn." His voice trembles as though he is about to shatter into pieces. "Now!"

"But Lorkan, Kaia..."

He barks then, his face flooding with anger. "NOW!"

I focus all of my energy. Anger, fear, and every other emotion boiling through my blood erupts inside of my chest. With a sonic boom, both of our bodies tear through the sky. I clench my fists, feeling my muscles tear as I carry us to Brawnwyn. A pulsing pain grows above my left eye, but I can't stop. If I stop, we fall. If we fall, we die. If we die, Lorkan dies. Brawnwyn falls. Fenrir is overtaken by Staxeons. Or worse, completely destroyed.

I cannot let that happen.

I will not let that happen.

CHAPTER 13

The door Scarface shoves us through is wooden and not something I've ever seen before. It opens into a familiar large cement room, and I only recognize it when I see the huddle of people against one end of the hold. We're in a stronghold.

"Took you long enough," a voice growls. A short and stocky, tan-skinned Staxeon with the trademark white tattoo stretching across his face like flames approaches Scarface. There are at least fifteen other Staxeons holding pistols and swords, standing near the group of scared people at the end of the hold. My eyes move over their tattooed faces, and then I look at the faces of the people huddled together anxiously. They're familiar. Too familiar. We *were* walking in circles.

"Mommy!"

Kaia doesn't hesitate before running toward the dark-haired child, but she doesn't get far with her shackled ankles. The giant Staxeon wraps a meaty arm around her waist and pulls her off of her feet. She screams; Greta runs faster toward her mother. I attempt to run to Greta, hoping to grab her before one of the Staxeons do, but I'm hit with a white-hot pain in my shoulder.

The force of the hit stops me in my tracks. It takes several long seconds for me to bring my head down to look at what hit me. My shoulder is dark red with blood dripping down my arm. The hole is small, but throbbing, and soon the pain spreads like lightning across my body.

"Lorkan!" Kaia's voice sounds farther away than it actually is. A flood of voices and shrieks erupts, but I can't make out any of the words. I think someone yells "Idiot" and something about being crazy. An arm gets wrapped around my neck and I'm pulled to the ground. A Staxeon snatches Greta, and the little girl fights and screams to no avail. Kaia's voice breaks through the dull roar of sounds; "Greta! No! Leave her alone! Leave her alone!"

With that, the pain and shock of my wound gets smothered by my anger. I thrash violently against the Staxeon holding me down.

"Get her out of here! Now! The Defender's out front! Go!" Scarface shouts. Greta is carried out of the hold. The Residents start shouting and trying to reach for the girl, but the Staxeons aim their weapons at them. Kaia fights against the giant, smashing her elbows and fists into his chest and arms as best as her shackled wrists allow. The arm around my neck tightens. I lift my arm and bring my elbow down on the Staxeon's knee. I slam my head backward into his face, and snatch the pistol from his holster.

The first shot goes into the giant's thigh. He roars in pain and drops to the floor. Kaia lands gracefully on her feet before driving her knee into the giant's face. The second and third shots go through the hands then knee of a Staxeon aiming his pistol at Kaia. I fire the fourth, fifth, and sixth shots at the Staxeons lifting their weapons at me, hitting their hands and wrists with every shot.

All those training sessions with Queen Thestera are finally paying off.

"Lorkan!" I don't know who shouted my name, but I drop and roll to my side. A steel blade clangs loudly against the cement floor beside my head. I lift the pistol and the seventh discharge moves cleanly through Scarface's thigh. A rapid chain of blasts echoes through the hold. I turn to see Kaia wielding the firing auto-pistol at the fleeing Staxeons. She is having difficulty holding it properly with her hands shackled together. I scramble to my feet and run toward her.

"Kaia, stop!" I shout over the blasts. The sound has hardly faded when she turns her big green eyes to me.

"They have Greta! They took my daughter!" She says something else but I can't understand her through the sobs.

"I know. I know. We'll get her back." I look over at the Residents as they nervously get to their feet. "Bind every Staxeon with whatever you can find," I announce. "Take away their weapons. We need to unlock these shackles." I walk over to Scarface. He's still writhing on the floor holding his thigh and growling in pain.

"I have a feeling you're the one with the key," I say as I aim the pistol at his face.

"Godless creature," he hisses. "You will be punished for this. God will punish you."

"Right now, God is letting me aim this pistol in your face. I don't think he's very concerned about you." A flicker of fear moves across his face and his eyes dart down for a brief instant. I squat beside him, keeping the pistol aimed at him, and reach into the pouch secured to his knee. I pull out the shiny, silver key and smile kindly at him. "May God have mercy on your soul."

I lose my balance once my elbow has cracked into his nose. He's unconscious and I struggle to not fall flat onto my face. A Resident by the name of Felton unlocks the shackles on my ankles and wrists, and helps me to my feet.

"How's your shoulder?" he asks me.

I had forgotten about the pistol wound in my shoulder. It doesn't hurt nearly as much as it did, and I can still lift and move my arm well enough. "It's okay, thanks. Everyone who is able needs to grab these pistols, bind the Staxeons, and be prepared for any intruders that are not Brawnwyn guards."

"There's a reason I'm not out helping protect the castle with the other young and able-bodied men," Felton replies weakly.

I put a hand on his small shoulder. "You're meant to stay here and protect them. I know you can, Felton. Don't let me down."

A small smile forms on the elderly man's face. He nods and walks over to the other Residents. I run to Kaia, unshackling her ankles and wrists. She snatches a new auto pistol from the floor, and I do the same.

"What's The Defender? That's where they were taking her," she says through sniffles. I open my mouth to answer her question, but I decide against it. I know telling a mother that her child has just been taken to a giant machine used to fight invaders from other worlds cannot possibly make her feel better. Especially when that giant machine was programmed to be used only by Prince Callum since he was deemed powerful enough to control it.

"I don't know, but we'll find her, Kaia," I assure her instead. "Seal off this door once we leave," I tell Felton.

The doors exiting the stronghold open to the main armory of Brawnwyn Castle. It is usually full of weaponry and armor, but at this moment it is completely empty. Every pistol and shred of armor has been removed; the cases that enclose the weapons have been shattered or haphazardly opened. I wave Kaia over to the far right exit that opens to a corridor where three Staxeons are fighting two castle guards. I fire two shots into the backs of Staxeon thighs, and Kaia hits the third Staxeon in his torso. They drop to the ground and the guards overtake them quickly. Kaia has already made her way through the exit to the front of the castle while I ask the guards if they're all right. They answer breathlessly and nod.

"The Defender," one begins as he swallows hard. I read the fear on his face and my heart sinks. "They've brought it from Fort Helm. It's out front."

"There are Staxeons in the stronghold. Make sure they're immobile and make sure the Residents are safe," I instruct.

They nod. "Yes, sir. You should be careful out there, sir. There's too many of them."

My stomach tightens. How many is too many, exactly? I dread seeing that number, but I need to get out there and find Kaia. "Protect the Residents," I repeat and I move cautiously through the exit.

They were not exaggerating.

CHAPTER 14

"When I told Gilbert to secure you in the Guard Tower, I did *not* mean like this," I growl for the umpteenth time as I reload my auto rifle and take aim at the group of Staxeons approaching. The weapon punches into my shoulder with every squeeze of the trigger, but my accuracy is unaffected. I can hear the shots fire off behind me in the opposite direction. She is completely ignoring me now. Better than her first response of a scoff and mumbled "Yeah, right."

That's where her son gets it from.

Another round discharges from her weapon. "This is *exactly* where I should be," she finally replies. "Defending my people. And my home." Another shot. "And you know I'm nowhere near as good at hand-to-hand combat."

"That's true," I mumble.

"I heard that, Agent," Thestera says as she aims through her scope. I don't mention that I had made no attempt in hiding my comment as her finger squeezes the trigger and she no doubt hits her mark.

"Staxeons are pulling weapons from the armory! I repeat, Staxeons are pulling heavy artillery from the armory. Proceed with caution," Officer Gilbert announces into my ear.

I tap my ear piece; "Seal the armory. It should have been sealed when this started."

"We did seal it, sir. Someone let them inside."

I do *not* need this shit right now. On top of the Staxeon uprising decimating Brawnwyn, there are traitors on our side aiding their cause. Someone is letting them into the armory. I've seen more than a few soldiers in Fenrir uniforms killing other soldiers rather than Staxeons.

"Have you heard from Cal?" Thestera breaks into my inner-dialogue.

I hate having to answer that question truthfully, but lying to her is far worse. "No, I haven't." She is silent for a long while. The only sound filling the room is that of our discharged weapons every few seconds. "I'm sure he's all right, Thestera. He's strong."

"I know." She pauses. Another round projects from her weapon. "Now, what are we going to do about The Defender?"

This Guard Tower stands in the center of Brawnwyn's expansive land. The topmost floor – where Thestera and I are – is built of reinforced steel specifically for snipers to do their job. There is only one entrance which I am guarding as Staxeons attempt to charge through the staircase. A steel table sits in the center of the room with weapons and ammunitions neatly organized on its surface. This room was constructed to allow no more than two people to enter the room at a time, allowing another soldier to stand guard and not be overpowered. This is a prime location for someone of Thestera's talents, and she has no doubt incapacitated almost forty Staxeons at this point. This is also an ideal location to see almost all of Brawnwyn, although The Defender is detracting slightly from the view.

The last update I received on The Defender was when it had been completed about two years ago. The file sent to me was extensive and included all of the metrics of its size, materials, capabilities, and overall power. The twenty-one hundred foot machine towers over the castle and casts a menacing shadow. I was riding on my speed cycle to Brawnwyn with the rest of my team when I saw it being carried by four air ships. It knocked over several trees during its flight. I could hardly believe they had managed to bring it over here. But the most pressing question that continues to roll over in my mind is what *exactly* do the Staxeons plan on doing with The Defender? It was programmed to be controlled only by Callum, so what else could be done with it? Other than block out the sun.

"I don't know what they could be planning with it, but it can't — TO THE RIGHT!"

I roll over my left shoulder and slam my back against the wall as the shrapnel missile flies by my head into the opposite wall. Thestera is already firing her rifle at the Staxeons pouring into the room. But we don't have enough time for her to take them all down before the missile releases the shrapnel.

Pushing off the wall behind me, I sprint toward Thestera at the opposite side of the room. I slide beneath the steel table and flip it onto its side with a loud crash and clang from the weapons and ammunition colliding to the floor. I drop my weapon to take hold of the table legs with both hands, and drag it between us and the missile imbedded in the wall. The missile shatters and shrapnel shoots in every direction. Pieces of metal puncture Staxeon bodies and dent into the steel table. I jump at the sound of the rifle discharging from underneath my arms holding the table in place.

Thestera lowers her weapon slowly. "I'm guessing they didn't know what that missile did."

"Thankfully for us," I reply as I stand and move toward the doorway. The staircase is empty – for now – but who knows how many more will flood this room. And who knows what weapons they will bring with them. "We need to leave this tower. Hold you up somewhere else."

"You're not hiding me away in that strong hold. I'm fighting."

I want to groan and roll my eyes, both of which I do while my back is to her. "You won't go in the strong hold. Just somewhere not so exposed and obvious." A pistol is equipped to my thigh, a fully-loaded auto is strapped to my back, and stun gloves are pulled onto my hands as Thestera reloads her rifle.

"Follow me," I say, but my voice is drowned out. A sound similar to that of an airship but at a significantly higher volume fills the air.

Thestera and I slap our hands over our ears to shut out as much of the noise as possible. I never heard or saw The Defender come to life, but I knew immediately that it was the source of the discord. We look outside at the towering machine as it stands straighter, squaring its monstrous shoulders and illuminating the visor acting as its eyes.

"Cal!" Thestera yells as she squeezes my arm. A wave of relief washes over me; this battle is about to be over.

Lines all over The Defender glow white like luminescent veins. Its visor turns from white-blue to purple as its head turns slightly toward the Guard Tower. Memories of the detailed report on The Defender flood my mind with particular facts coming to the forefront. The most prevalent fact being The Defender's attack mechanism within its visor. This mechanism causes the light within the visor to change from white to a dark purple color before unleashing a devastating beam of energy. This beam is strong enough to annihilate even the sturdiest and most well-built structures, regardless of the materials used to construct them. Metal and steel melt, iron disintegrates, even diamond shatters under its blast. This mechanism was built to destroy foreign invaders from other planets.

And it is focusing that mechanism on us.

"MOVE! MOVE!"

Thestera's petite body is in my arms as I pull her to the doorway. We won't make it. We won't get out of this tower before The Defender destroys it. But instinct is telling me to try anyway.

Cal is *not* in that machine. And Brawnwyn, and most likely all of Fenrir, is going to learn what The Defender is capable of in the worst possible way.

CHAPTER 15

A couple of years ago, Rhett had alerted me to the completion of The Defender. He sent me the files on its specific details, everything from its height and weight to each individual part involved in its function. The Defender was built to allow me – and only me—to operate it by sensing my unique blood code. Being Prince of Fenrir, son of King Caderyn, and someone gifted with hyper-human capabilities, I was entrusted with the operation and use of The Defender. And it was created to be used for the sole purpose of fighting foreign invaders, should they be foolish enough to return.

The most important pieces of information I needed from the file Rhett sent me were: 1) the energy and damage The Defender could administer; 2) the energy it required to operate; and 3) the damage it could cause to me while operating it.

Knowing full well that this machine can tear through air ships and solar cannons like fingers through a hologram, that it can level a city with the misuse of a thruster engine, that it is capable of destroying an entire planet should enough energy be focused, I still insist on flying right into its line of vision.

Also known as its line of impending destruction.

I curl my fist and regret my decision as soon as I've made it, but no other ideas are coming to mind. My knuckles connect with the visor but cause no damage to the machine's structure. The bones in my hand, however, break immediately. The pain surges up my arm and shoulder.

The Defender has been distracted from destroying Brawnwyn, which was my intention. But now Reinhardt and I are falling out of the sky. I try to lift us, slow us down, anything, but the pain above my left eye has grown across my entire skull and it's not allowing me to use my power. An arm wraps around my torso, pulling my hand into my chest which sends a vicious swell of pain through me. Another arm slips around my waist. Reinhardt's chest presses against my back and he manages to turn us so that I'm looking up at The Defender as we plummet to the ground.

The cracking sound of us hitting the ground explodes into my ears and is quickly followed by a whistle as we slide rapidly on a cold, slick surface. We hit a wall and Reinhardt helps me to my feet.

"Good thinking," I croak with my eyes fixed on the ice slide that eased our way to the ground. I grimace at my hand and look back up at The Defender scanning the ground for us.

"How do we get her out of there?" Reinhardt asks. I open my mouth to ask who is powering The Defender when a high-pitched howl cuts through the air. The projectile explodes on contact with The Defender, letting out a burst of flames and a plume of dark smoke.

"GRETA!" Reinhardt yells. That is who is inside the machine, and she matters to Reinhardt. Another projectile soars through the air and collides into The Defender. It, too, leaves barely a scratch on the machine.

Reinhardt turns his icy glare to me. "They have to stop firing! Get them to stop firing at her!"

I tap my ear piece; "Rhett! Rhett, can you hear me?"

"Cal?!"

"Rhett, you need to order them to stop firing at The Defender."

"Are you inside it?"

Before I can answer, an explosion bursts through the dull roar of battle surrounding us. The Defender has shattered an airship into dust and smoke.

"No, that's not me in there. I don't know who it is."

"There's a child inside," Reinhardt tells me. "My child. My daughter. Please," he turns his gaze back to the machine. Its visor begins to glow blue and darken. "Please, get her out of there," he pleads.

Daughter? Reinhardt's daughter? The idea of him even having a daughter makes me forget how to speak for a moment. I have completely missed what Rhett was barking into my ear.

"Cal?!"

"Yes! I'm here. Stop them from firing at it." Reinhardt takes a hold of my shattered hand and wrist; I growl through clenched teeth as his hands glow silvery-white. Ice cracks and spreads across my skin. The cold is numbing and the pain subsides drastically. "There is a little girl inside," I conclude as Reinhardt releases my frozen hand.

"What? How?"

"Questions will be answered *after* we save her, Rhett!" I bark. "Right now you need to stop them from firing at her."

"Okay, done. How do we stop it?"

That is one question that needs to be answered now.

"As the Head of Brawnwyn's Guard, aren't *you* supposed to be the one with the ideas?"

There is a deafening howl from over our heads. A blue blast of energy emanates from The Defender's visor and decimates through one of the spires of the castle. The stone structure is turned into a dusty powder cascading over the ground in a thick grey cloud.

"First," Rhett says into my ear, "we need to get it away from the castle before it does any further damage!"

"Agreed. I'm on it." I turn to Reinhardt, but he is no longer standing beside me. He is barreling through a crowd of Staxeons with frozen fists, charging toward one point. I do not have time to follow him.

I turn back toward The Defender as its visor begins to glow blue again. Greta is not strong enough to bring about the most destructive level of the visor, and that is one of the *few* things working on our side at the moment. That and how long it is taking for the visor to recharge before another blast can be produced. She is too small and young to use The Defender to its full potential. Which also means this machine will overwhelm her a lot faster, which makes time of the essence.

A Staxeon aims a pistol at me; I extend my hand and shove the weapon into his face. The pain above my eye shoots like lightning across my skull. I slam my hand against my forehead and grimace. My knees buckle and I drop to the ground, struggling to keep my face from colliding into the stone. Warm wetness trickles from my nose and onto my lips; I know it's blood before I wipe it away with the back of my hand.

A cold blade touches my throat, lifting my gaze up to a Brawnwyn guard. He is scowling at me as he forces me to sit on my heels. He looks familiar, but I can't place him. My head is pounding angrily. I don't believe I have enough strength to fight this one. Or any others who may follow him.

"Where's your power now, Your Highness?" he hisses. The face blurs into recognition: Officer Den. The guard I locked in Reinhardt's cell. I traded one Staxeon for another. I would laugh if my head was not threatening to explode. "Perhaps Staxos has saw fit to punish your heresy," he says.

I reach for my sword, but I'm moving too slowly. The pain growing behind my eyes and down my neck is hindering all bodily control, and when the explosive pop bursts through my ears, the pain drops me to the ground and into darkness. A loud beep howls through my brain. I have finally done it. I have ruptured enough blood vessels to cause my entire head to explode. But then the throbbing pain returns in a dull pulse, gaining strength and agony with each second. I can't be dead since I'm still in pain, unless this is truly the worst incarnation of Hell one could ever be thrown into.

"Cal!"

The voice sounds miles away and under water. The darkness is fading and I can see blurred colors and silhouettes of objects. The sound washes through my mind again, and I slowly turn my pounding head toward its origin. Arms are around me immediately and I feel something soft pressing against my forehead and face. Oddly, the pain is subsiding. By the time my face is cradled in soft yet strong hands, my vision is almost completely restored to normal. His eyes are big and brown and full of concern. My body recognizes him before my brain does, slipping my arms around him and leaning my chest toward him. I touch his face and his chocolate brown hair. His mouth is moving but the sound is faded and I'm not really paying attention to what he's saying.

Lorkan pulls my arm around his shoulders and lifts me effortlessly onto my feet. The pain in my head has diminished significantly, and I am able to actually walk where he is pulling me. He leans me against a cold, hard surface and my brain instantly thinks it's another ice creation by Reinhardt. I slowly glance over my shoulder and notice it is the stone wall of the castle gates.

"Are you okay?" he asks me with his hand gently holding my chin.

My body sinks toward him and I hug him tightly. "Lorkan," I breathe. He smells of blood and dirt; he feels warm, but there's something sticky beneath my fingertips. I pull back to see the bloody wound in his shoulder. "No, no, no," I mutter repeatedly.

"I'm okay. I'm okay, Cal. Cal! I'm okay," he replies. He has to take hold of my shoulders and force me to look up at him to know he is telling me the truth. His eyes then dart down to my ice-encased hand. "What happened to your hand?"

"I...broke it," I answer lamely. I had forgotten all about my frozen wrist and fingers. "It's okay."

"Kaia's daughter is in The Defender," he says. "I couldn't get to her in time."

"Kaia's daughter?" Lorkan nods in response. "The Resident taken with you? Greta is her daughter?" He nods again with a slightly perplexed look on his face. "Well that explains everything." I look into his big brown eyes as he pushes his long, sticky hair out of the way. "I need my crown. That's the only way I'll be strong enough to stop The Defender and get her out of there." My head throbs in response to my plan, reminding me of just how weak I am.

"I'll get your crown," Lorkan says, pressing a hand to my chest to keep me still. "Stay here and don't die." He holds my chin and kisses me. I have missed that far too much, and I've almost forgotten there is a war happening around us and a giant machine threatening to destroy everything.

"Be careful," I manage to tell him. He kisses me again before running toward the castle entrance. I tap my ear piece. "Rhett." I pull my hilt from against my hip and the black viscous blade grows.

"Cal, I'm here," he answers.

"Whenever the visor on The Defender glows blue, fire a missile right by its head. Do *not* hit it, just distract it enough to not fire."

"Will do," he replies.

"Cal!" Reinhardt runs over to me holding the hand of a brunette with a narrow face and bright green eyes stained red with tears.

"Are you all right?" the woman asks. I can only imagine what she is seeing. The Prince of Fenrir looking near death with a frozen hand and a skull several sizes too big.

I manage a nod. "Lorkan is getting my crown. Then I will be able to get your daughter out of there." The woman's – Kaia, I guess – eyes glisten with fresh tears.

"Thank you," she whimpers.

A missile bursts near The Defender. Reinhardt and Kaia turn toward the sound. "They're not firing at her. Just distracting her so she can't fire the energy blasts."

"What happens if they hit her?" Kaia asks.

Her shiny green eyes bounce from Reinhardt to me and back again. I do not want to answer that question. Thankfully, Reinhardt answers it for me.

"It will make her angry and she could destroy everything." His eyes flicker to me, and I obey the unspoken request. The truth will not help Kaia or Greta. "I'll lead her toward Namor," he adds then. He turns to Kaia and kisses her before she protests. "I *will* bring her back." He turns to me. "You better catch up soon."

He runs toward The Defender and creates another slide of ice, gliding him into the air. I bring my eyes to Kaia; tears are streaming down her face as she watches Reinhardt and The Defender.

"You should take shelter in the strong hold."

She shakes her head. "No, Your Highness. I need to stay as close to her as I can."

I nod and push away from the wall. Kaia extends her hands to me. "I got it. My strength is coming back." That is not a complete lie. My sword is not as heavy now. My head feels closer to its regular size. The pain is no longer a sharp, electric web setting fire to every inch of my scalp, but more of a dull throbbing. And Staxeons are approaching with heavy artillery.

"Get behind me," I instruct Kaia with my arm guiding her backward.

The auto-pistols are leveled at our faces. I keep my sword behind me, hiding the blade as it grows and expands to the ground, reaching over five feet in length. Before the first trigger is squeezed by the second Staxeon from the right, I have already pushed off of the ground toward them and slid my blade through his stomach. I turn my blade, tearing through his torso to cut through the three Staxeons standing beside him. I smash my elbow into the right man's jaw before cutting him down.

Another lightning strike of pain shoots from the base of my skull up and over to my forehead. My vision darkens and I stab my sword into the ground, hoping it will keep me propped up. A voice calls my name, and several explosions pop around me. Blinking several times as the aching in my head subsides, my blade liquefies into a whip. Its tail wraps around the ankles of an approaching Staxeon, tearing him off of his feet. I crack it at the pistol held by another before spinning it around her throat and slamming her to the ground.

"Cal!"

I turn to Lorkan's voice. He shoves the heel of his hand into someone's face and cracks his elbow into the face of another as he runs toward me holding the familiar dark grey crown. The explosion of the energy blast from The Defender turns my attention toward Namor Forest and the massive machine following Reinhardt to it. Trees fall and black smoke billows into the sky.

I do not notice Lorkan standing beside me or even feel him put the cold, heavy object on my head. It is not until the wave of energy and power floods through my muscles do I even realize what has just happened. The throbbing pain in my head vanishes immediately, disappearing into its origin point above my left eye. The ice around my left hand shatters, and my fingers stretch and move as the bone heals into one solid piece.

I turn to Lorkan; "Thanks. Find Rhett and my mom." I point a finger at him; "Do *not* die."

The mental energy coursing through my veins sends me into the air with an explosion of dirt and dust around me. I weave through The Defender's legs and see Reinhardt on the ground slamming his ice-covered fists into the machine. Each hit shatters the ice on his knuckles, but does not even cause a dent in The Defender. The machine's foot lifts into the air and drops fast onto Reinhardt. I sweep in beside him, snatching him out of the way. A plume of dust bursts around us as I fly into the air with Reinhardt panting heavily beside me.

"You sure took your time," he growls. I resist the urge to drop him. "How do we get her out?"

"Still working on that part," I answer as we glide around the machine's visor as it attempts to follow us.

"Work faster!" Reinhardt barks.

I need to figure out the weak spots on this machine, but I know there are not many. The file Rhett had sent me when the machine was completed had so much information, I could barely get through its most important details. I read through what mattered to me: the power and the consequences. I don't remember much of the consequences of using The Defender, but I know they exist. And I know they have to be significant for Greta if they exist at all for me.

Lorkan would remember every detail about The Defender. He was more interested in that thousand-paged manual than I was. I caught him several times reading through it, examining every detail, sometimes explaining in excitement the information he read. *Should you be so inclined, you could destroy an entire planet with this machine,* he said once while laying on my bed. *I don't think God has that much power.* It was funny then. But now, I need to know exactly what was in that file and only Lorkan will remember it.

I tap my ear piece; "Rhett, I need you."

"Where are you?" Rhett answers immediately.

"Leading The Defender away from the castle," I answer. "Has Lorkan found you?"

"No. Lorkan is here?"

"Yes. Find him."

"MOVE!" Reinhardt shouts.

The shield created by my mental power wraps around us an instant before The Defender's energy blast hits. The metallic clang of the blast hitting the invisible wall rings out; the light emanated is nearly blinding. Reinhardt and I are thrown backward, and the psychic bubble surrounding us breaks through trees and slams into the ground.

A shadow overtakes us as The Defender lifts its foot above. I lift my sword over our heads as it widens into a flat, black shield. Upon the force of the fallen attachment, I am forced into the ground sending up an eruption of dirt around me. My muscles lock and my power flares as I push against The Defender. It staggers backward as a projectile explodes into its side. The missiles are being launched from Brawnwyn.

"Rhett! Don't hit her!" I bark into the ear piece.

"It's not us! Staxeons must have a hold of the cannons." He growls something incoherent. "Handling it," he grunts.

The Defender turns its attention toward Brawnwyn, aiming its glowing visor back at the castle. I focus all of my energy on wrapping around the machine; my hands extend and pull back as though tugging on the reins of a runaway horse. My feet bury into the ground, dragging along the machine as it fights against my hold. The shining piece of ice shatters upon impact with the smooth, metal surface of the machine. Its gaze returns to us and the visor glows.

"Cal, I found Lorkan," Rhett says into my ear; he grunts again and swears angrily.

"Put him on." I pull Reinhardt and myself into the air before the glowing visor can expel its blast.

"Cal, it's me."

"Lorkan, please tell me you remember the weak spots on The Defender. From the files Rhett sent me." We dip around the machine's swinging limb and hover behind it.

I hear a grunt and gunfire; my heart stops beating for a moment until I hear Lorkan's voice again. "Yes, um, yeah, yeah. The Achilles

Heel, behind the legs of The Defender. If you can break through the metal, you can disable—Agh!"

"Lorkan!"

"I'm—I'm fine. Behind the legs of The Defender you can disable the connection of the machine to Greta. You have to cut through the steel plate to reach the blood-binding."

"That won't hurt her?" I ask. Reinhardt looks at me with panicked eyes as the psychic bubble surrounding us intercepts a missile from hitting The Defender.

"No, not *really*," he answers reluctantly. "How long she's in there without the connection is what could cause the damage. You need to move fast. The Defender will start to rebuild the connection, and that could hurt her worse than actually cutting through it."

"Got it." I turn to Reinhardt. "I'm going to sever the connection The Defender has on Greta, and we will get her out of there. But we need to move fast."

Without another word we plummet to the ground. Reinhardt lets out a string of swears before we land on our feet. The Defender steps backward to find us, aiming its glowing visor down at the ground. Reinhardt runs and I hear the ice cracking as it formulates into a shimmering orb in his palm. He fires it at the front of the machine, distracting it long enough to keep it from moving. I plunge the black blade of my sword through the steel panel. The point of the blade flattens and spreads in either direction, allowing me to pull the panel off of The Defender. The machine pulls its limb away from me. I extend my hand and crush the luminescent connectors with my power.

An ear-splitting shrieking noise tears through the air and silences just as quickly. The illuminated veins across The Defender's frame dim and darken, but they do not extinguish completely. Now is my only moment before the machine reconnects to Greta. I push off the ground and launch into the air. As I ascend closer to where Greta is held within the machine, I glide the black blade through the dimly lit steel. I pull my hand back, ripping the steel wall away to see the small child inside.

Her head is lolled to the side with a mop of dark brown hair strewn across her face. The veins in her arms have darkened like burns on her pale skin. She is breathing softly and her eyes are struggling to open. I pull her carefully from the steel cage and cradle her against my chest. Once the machine has lost its power source, the lights deaden and a low buzz sounds its killed functionality. Greta and I drift slowly to the ground.

Reinhardt's eyes are brimming with tears as I hand his daughter to him. He presses her against his chest and kisses her head. "Greta," he whispers. "Greta?"

She makes a little whimpering sound and moves her head slightly. "Daddy," she manages to croak. He lifts his red-stained eyes to me.

"Thank you. Thank you, Cal."

I don't respond. My mouth is dry, my throat is tight, and I can hardly breathe in enough air to formulate words. All I can do is nod. A respectful nod with my mouth in a thin line that slightly resembles a smile. Something won't allow me to verbalize any response. It fears if I open my mouth, regretted words will come tumbling out. Words that may admit how similar Reinhardt and I are. Words that need not be spoken.

CHAPTER 16

I plant my knee firmly into the back of the squirming Staxeon as I shackle his wrists together. He's growling something about taking back what is theirs as he writhes beneath me. I don't bother letting him know that he will most likely be spending the rest of his life in a jail cell beneath Brawnwyn Castle, and whatever it is he thinks belongs to him won't be his anytime soon.

"I'll take him," a petite guard says as she walks over to me. Her dark hair is matted to her face and neck; her uniform is dirty and torn. She grips his arm and lifts him onto his feet with a strong tug before I can even offer assistance.

"Officer Gilbert," Rhett says to the guard dragging the Staxeon away. She turns back to look at him. "Put as many of the prisoners in the cells under the castle."

"There are only eighteen cells, sir. We don't have nearly enough space," she replies.

"We'll find space for them. Fill the cells here, then we'll fill each cell in every city until they are all locked up where they belong. We'll *make* space," Rhett answers.

Officer Gilbert nods and the corner of her mouth turns up slightly. She yanks the prisoner along with her, and other guards lead more Staxeons to the cells. Rhett turns to me and arches a dark red eyebrow. His jaw sets and he squares his shoulders. "You know it's *your* fault we have to find space for all of them. All because you refuse to decommission a few of them."

I shake my head slowly and scrunch my nose. "I can't kill anyone, Rhett."

His expression softens and an actual smile appears on his face, or at least the closest to a smile I have ever seen Rhett's face contort into. He squeezes my shoulder. "And I hope you never have to."

"Agent Ryckoff," a guard announces. "We caught her trying to escape through one of the secret emergency exits."

Rhett and I turn toward the guard. He is walking and pulling a woman beside him by her upper arm. Her wrists are shackled, her clothes are bloodied, and I can make out white markings peering out from underneath the tears in her shirt. The guard whips her around to face Rhett, and my face falls once I recognize the woman.

"Zoe?"

I spin around at the sound of Cal's voice. A dense fog of confusion is on his face. I jog over to him and our fingers interlock effortlessly. His dark blue hair is tousled about on his head with the crown acting as its barrier. His dark silver armor is covered in dust and blood; it is a drastic change from its usually spotless and shimmering form. He smiles gently at me then brings his eyes back to Zoe in the guards' custody.

She is scowling at all of us. Blood is dried at the corner of her mouth and she has a purple bruise forming on her cheek. Cal walks closer to her, bringing me along, and we stand beside Rhett.

"You released that footage of Cal," Rhett finally breaks through the deafening silence.

Footage? What footage?

"Alerting your people that I was out of the castle?" Cal adds, "So they could attack without me in their way. You were betraying us from the beginning." Something flickers across his face and he scoffs; "That explains how all of these Staxeons have guard uniforms and guard-grade weaponry."

"Also explains who was letting Staxeons into the armory when I had it locked down," Rhett adds between tight lips.

Cal's jaw clenches but I can see in his eyes that he is more saddened than angry. He trusted Zoe. *We* trusted Zoe. To think she was helping the Staxeons all along is difficult to accept. But now as I look at her, it becomes more and more obvious. Those white markings peering through her torn clothes are her white tattoos. I have never seen her in anything other than turtlenecks and long-sleeved tops; I have never seen the skin of her arms before because she was hiding her tattoos. She was hiding the truth. She was hiding in plain sight. Along with the rest of them.

"It is *you* who has betrayed Fenrir," she hisses at Cal. "*I* was loyal to Staxos, to the true God and true king of this realm. And He *will* return. And He *will* take back what is His."

I brace myself for the angry rant I know Cal is going to unleash. I can feel the heat radiating off of his skin. Cal has never been religious and has always had a strong disdain for those who allow it to overrule their reason. Now to see someone we all thought we knew to be blinded by the violent and angry side of religion, even I understand that Cal must have had enough of gods and their followers for ten lifetimes. I've had enough of them myself, to be honest.

But instead of a rant, he sighs. He lowers his head slightly and sighs. He lifts his eyes back to Zoe.

"I will not allow this realm to fall into the hands of those who cannot differentiate between faith and reason. The Staxos you worship is not a god I respect. I respect the god whom champions peace over tyranny. And I do not think your kind understand the difference."

I fight the urge to cheer at Cal's eloquent and calm response. I had no idea he was capable of speaking so rationally in the face of a radical's religious beliefs. But that is just one of the many reasons I'm in love with this man: he's always surprising me. So instead of cheering or howling with appreciation, I just squeeze his hand to remind him I am always by his side.

Cal only says "Rhett," and the Head of Castle Security orders the guards to take Zoe away to an airship where she will be locked into a cell at Fort Helm. Cal watches as she is led away.

"She helped them get into the castle," he says quietly. "She showed them the sub-level entrances. Gave them access to all of that weaponry. She helped start all of this death and destruction…because of her beliefs."

I rub his back and lower my head to kiss his temple. "You couldn't have known, Cal."

"I let her into this castle."

"Don't do this to yourself. You couldn't have known. None of us knew. She hid it well because that was her intention."

I struggle to find the right words to say. None of this sounds right or helpful. Cal is silent. I finally take a deep breath and pull Cal to face me. His green eyes lift to meet mine.

"You are the prince and future king this realm needs. And you will lead us back to peace. I know it." His face softens slightly and a hint of a smile appears on his lips.

"Thank you," he whispers.

I glance around us to make sure we aren't being overheard. Rhett is speaking with a group of guards, gesturing to the shackled prisoners lying on the castle floor. I bring my focus back to Cal.

"Is Greta okay?" I ask quietly.

Cal nods, "Yeah. We got her out before The Defender did too much damage. I think she will be okay."

I breathe a sigh of relief. I can only imagine how happy Kaia must be now that Greta is safe. I drop my hand on Cal's shoulder. "Thank God. Where are they? I want to make sure they both get seen by the doctors. Make sure Greta is okay."

He shakes his head slowly. "They…they're gone."

"Gone?"

Cal lowers his voice and steps closer to me. His hand holds the back of my head and his fingers comb through the hair at the base of my skull. His fingers feel cool against my sticky, hot skin.

"I told Reinhardt to go. I told him to take Greta and Kaia and go. If they stayed here, Reinhardt would be put back in that cell." He shakes his head slowly and his eyes lower for a brief moment. "It...wouldn't be right."

A part of me is saddened that I couldn't say good-bye to them. That I didn't get to make sure Greta and Kaia were okay. But it only takes one look at Cal's dirty and pained face for me to smile at him. I lean forward to kiss him, but Queen Thestera calling his name loudly and running toward us stops me. We both turn to face her as she approaches quickly, her arms already open to sweep Cal into them. Their armor clangs loudly when she collides into him. She kisses his head and squeezes him; she did similar to me when we reunited earlier.

"I'm so glad you're safe," I hear her whisper. She pulls back and looks at me, placing a hand gingerly against my cheek. "I'm so glad *both* of my boys are safe."

"Your Majesty, Your Highness," Rhett steps up beside me. "I'm sending out our remaining forces to secure the other cities besieged by Staxeons. I'm going with the team to Fort Helm. Make sure Zoe gets the smallest and most cramped cell they have available."

"I would like to go with you," Cal says at the same time a man's voice says "Your Majesty" from behind Thestera.

"As would I," I add to Rhett. He gives me a surprised look and Cal opens his mouth to say something – protest, no doubt—but he quickly closes it and clenches his jaw instead. I squeeze his hand. "I think it best we stick together."

"I can't say I disagree," he replies.

"No, that's absurd," Thestera says to the round-faced man she's speaking to.

"Mom? What's wrong?"

She looks at Cal, at me, then back to Cal. Her brows are knitted above her pale green eyes. "The High Court wants to try you for freeing the Staxeon prisoner."

"No."

I don't know where or from whom that response came until everyone turns to look at me. Cal squeezes my hand. I open my mouth to apologize, but no sound comes out. I just look awkwardly at everyone's faces before lowering my eyes to Cal.

"It's okay," he says to me first. Then he turns to Thestera and the round-faced man beside her. "I need to answer for my actions. All I ask is that I aid in clearing the besieged cities before my trial. Can the High Court amend to that?"

"I will discuss it with them, sir," the man replies. "I'm sure they will adhere to the request." He nods, "Your Majesty, Your Highness," and walks away briskly.

"This isn't fair," Thestera whispers through a cracking voice. Her eyes are shining and turning red.

"Mom, it's the law."

"Well, it's ridiculous, and I complained to Deryn when he decreed it."

I wrap my arm around the queen and pull her against me. Rhett, Cal, and I exchange looks. Cal nods to Rhett whom turns without a word and heads toward the entryway of the castle. Cal slips his arm around his mom and places his other hand on my back.

"I have to help Rhett and the others…and the people who need us," he says softly.

She nods slowly and sniffles. "I know you do," she croaks. Then she scoffs; "Just like your father. Helping everyone else before himself."

"He taught me well," Cal replies with a smile.

Thestera takes a deep breath and stands straight. She squares her shoulders and wipes the tears from her cheeks. Just like that, she's back to being powerful Queen of Fenrir whom does not allow emotions to get the best of her.

"You're absolutely right, the people of Fenrir need us. We will.. " she sighs, "deal with the High Court later." She holds Cal's chin in her hand; "Be careful out there." She turns to me and grabs my chin, taking me by surprise. "That goes for you, too. And that goes double for Rhett. He won't have me protecting him out there." She grins.

"We'll handle that," I tell her.

She nods again and turns to walk away as more bustling assistants and public relations handlers appear around her.

"Mom, wait," Cal speaks up. He pulls his bladeless hilt from his side and hands it to her. "Could you take this for me? I…will not be needing it."

"Hopefully you never will again," she replies softly before walking away.

Cal turns to me. "Wishful thinking."

"It could happen," I reply, although I know it isn't likely. Wars are always going to be happening. no matter how adamantly we strive for peace. But it isn't completely unfathomable that the most powerful weapon in the realm will not have to draw blood again.

I'll keep hoping for that.

CHAPTER 17

"Prince Callum, you stand accused of freeing a prisoner from within Brawnwyn Castle. This accusation is the result of visual footage taken from Brawnwyn Castle's security and displayed on the Internet for the realm to see. How do you plead to this accusation?"

The High Court is made up of five judges appointed by the people of Fenrir. Every year there is a reelection, similar to the one that keeps my family as the reigning monarchy. The judge delivering the opening speech of the crime I am being tried for is a dark-haired man named Payne, which I hope is not some sort of an omen against me; he has been holding this seat for the past eighteen years.

The chamber we are in is a large, round room with pale walls and a skylight above our heads. Sunlight is pouring in, basking each of us in a golden glow. The judges are not actually seated in this room with me. Instead five holographic visual projections of them are seated in high-backed chairs and their names digitally written by their feet should I need to address any of them directly. There are three female judges (Frye, Nuñez-Pearson, Zou) and two male (Payne and Deshi). I stand in the center of the room about twelve feet away from the line of judges seated before me. Cameras are located in four points of the room sending a live feed of this hearing to the two news channels used strictly for messages from Brawnwyn. This is for the purpose of preventing any misconduct by the judges, myself, or any attempt at claiming injustice because of my title.

"I plead guilty, Judges," I answer.

They nod solemnly and look at one another. The word MUTED appears over each of their names; their mouths are moving but I hear no sound. They are discussing my sentencing and I can only stand there and wait for them to make their decision. I know I will not be getting any easier or harsher punishment because I am the Prince of Fenrir. I am to be treated like anyone else who broke the law, and I was expecting that. It is the main reason why my family continues to be elected into power every year. We stand to uphold justice and fairness regardless of what title a person may hold. If you are the Prince of Fenrir or a server in a bar in Old Trail Town, you will receive the same sentence for the same crime.

"Your Highness," Judge Zou says suddenly. I lift my eyes to her. The MUTED words have disappeared from the Judges' names. "For this crime, you are to be sentenced to two years imprisonment in the dungeon of Brawnwyn Castle."

I had asked Rhett what the sentence for freeing a prisoner was, and he did not shield me from the answer. It made my stomach knot, and Mom whimpered and fought back tears. Lorkan just squeezed my hand and his jaw clenched. I could see the fight bubbling up beneath the calm façade he often wore, but we both knew there was nothing we could do about it. Even Rhett looked bothered to have to answer such a question knowing it was what awaited me.

He said it would be two years, and yet hearing it officially from the High Court still knocked the air out of me slightly. I had thought about what it would be like to truly be in the dungeons beneath the castle for two years. To suddenly be treated as a criminal and sitting in that small cell every day for two years was a jarring reality, but it is one that I have earned. A younger version of me would have fought this, but I know I cannot. I know there is no use. And my father would not have fought it. *Justice is indestructible if we protect it,* he said to me when I asked him why he was so insistent on all citizens of Fenrir being tried exactly the same regardless of status. *Justice has to be blind to all differing factors. Only the crime should decide your punishment, not your name, money, or power. If we hope to protect justice, we have to enforce it, and we can never be above it.*

"Two days from today, Thursday, the fourth, at ten o'clock in the morning, you are to be processed into your cell. Exactly two years from that date is the end of your sentence," Judge Deshi explains. "From the start of your sentence to your release two years later, you are stripped of your title as Prince of Fenrir. You are to serve your sentence in its entirety unless unforeseen circumstances require your attention. Should that occur, your sentence will be suspended until the crisis has been handled, which will be promptly followed by the resumption of your sentence through to its completion. Do you understand the overview of your sentence, Your Highness?"

I nod; "Yes, Judges, I do."

"Before we dismiss you, Your Highness," Judge Frye says as she edges forward. "I speak on behalf of the High Court when I say that we respect and appreciate your service to this realm. We understand why you acted the way you did, and I doubt there are any of us seated before you today whom would have acted any differently should we had found ourselves in a similar situation. Your contributions toward protecting the people of Fenrir, and aiding in the culmination of the Staxeon uprising from cities across the realm has not gone unacknowledged."

A smile appears on my face and I nod. "Anything for the service of Fenrir. But thank you for your understanding, Judges."

"You are dismissed, Your Highness," Payne says finally.

With another nod from me and the judges, the holographic projections turn off one at a time. And just like that, my fate is sealed.

CHAPTER 18

"I feel as though I should be packing a bag, but… I'm not going on a trip. Just…away."

I turn to look at Rhett whom is seated in the oversized dark blue chair next to the window. His foot is resting on his knee, and his fingers are interlocked behind his russet-red head. He has been sitting in that very spot for the last hour as I have paced awkwardly around my room, moving things from one spot to another. Everything has been returned to their original locations.

Rhett leans forward, resting his elbows on his knees. "I know you're scared, Cal," he says. "But you're going to get through this. Two years will be over faster than you know. We will be visiting you every week. I will keep the realm safe, especially Lorkan and Thestera. Those two will not leave my sight, you can count on that."

I nod and sigh. "Thank you, Rhett. Where are Lorkan and my mom anyway? You would think they would be here panicking along with me." I run my hand through my hair and tug at the roots.

"The Queen had a meeting in Oceanside, but she should be returning any minute now," Rhett answers as he strides over to me. He plants his hands on my shoulders. "Callum, stop and take a breath."

"I seem to be struggling with that," I answer lamely.

"You are going to be fine. You're the Prince of Fenrir. When you were twelve you were capable of lifting entire vehicles with your mind. At fifteen you insisted on fighting the foreign invaders on your own. And merely days ago, you took down a machine created to be the most powerful weapon in this world. You're the strongest man I know, Callum, and you *will* get through this."

"Would you be uncomfortable if I hugged you?"

"Of course I will," he replies with a smirk. His arms wrap around me and squeeze me against his strong frame; he smells of leather and cologne. I refuse to cry; Rhett would not be able to handle it, and I have already pushed him far enough.

"Oh thank goodness, I haven't missed you!"

We both turn to face my mother as she scurries into the room and hugs me tightly. "I was terrified the meeting would run over and I wouldn't be able to see you off." Her eyes turn red and start to water already.

"You're seeing me, you're seeing me," I assure her with a hug. I will not admit I was wishing she was with me all along. That will only break her heart further, and there is no purpose in that. And I hate to admit that I need my mother as much as I do. That is not exactly what a twenty-six year-old prince should be declaring in the face of a prison sentence.

"Where's Lorkan?" she asks, wiping the tears from her eyes before they have fallen.

"I don't know," I answer. "I haven't seen him all morning."

His side of the bed was empty before I awoke. I do not admit how painful that has been. This is my last hour before I am sitting in the dungeon of Brawnwyn Castle for two years, and he is nowhere to be found. I expected him to be putting on a brave face beside me all morning. I expected him to be reassuring me everything was going to be okay. Instead, he has not been seen and Rhett was forced into those responsibilities.

"That's odd," she adds.

"Wait!" Lorkan shouts from down the corridor. "Cal, wait!"

I take long strides to the open doorway of my room. Lorkan practically collides into me. He is panting and has a hand pressed against my chest.

"Are you okay?" I ask him.

He nods. "Yeah, yeah," he pants. He stands straight and smiles brightly at me. "I wasn't going to miss you. I just…" He looks into my room at Rhett and my mom. "…I had to see someone off." He lowers his voice; "And he wanted me to give you this."

I move my eyes from Lorkan's big brown ones down passed his soft smile and black-bandaged shoulder to the folded paper in his hand. I take the paper from him and unfold it. It's a letter. A handwritten letter. I do not recall the last time I received a handwritten letter. That's not true, I do. It was from Lorkan back when we were teenagers and used to exchange notes throughout the day. Back when we were just friends.

But this letter was delivered by Lorkan yet not written by him. My eyes flicker down to the name at the bottom, then I bring them back up to the beginning.

Callum,

I have a feeling you are a lot like me in the sense that we do not handle face-to-face good-byes very well. We avoided it altogether, which is why this farewell is written.

I respect you accepting your sentence from the High Court. While I am inept with good-byes, thank-you's are a bit easier for me. However, I cannot thank you enough to equate to what you returned to me. My freedom being the smallest of these gifts. I never thought I would have the ability to watch Greta play outside, let alone grow up and live a life outside of the Staxeon radical hold.

She is doing well, by the way. She remembers some of what happened and has these dark scars on her arms, but none of that seems to bother her at all. She asked about you. She asked when she would see you again. Kaia has asked similar questions about Lorkan, hoping greatly to see him again one day. That is something we will have to determine in the future. Near future, hopefully.

I cannot adequately repay your actions with much of anything, but I can offer you a small piece of information for your sentence. While the security systems in the cells are extremely well engineered, there is one minor flaw. Should one be so inclined to short-circuit the coding screen, the cell door opens without hindering the heart monitor, allowing for visitors inside and undetected. I hope that information comes in use for you.

Thank you again for all that you did for my family and myself. Best of luck to you in the following two years.

I look forward to your return to the throne.

Reinhardt

I smile at the paper and lift my eyes back to Lorkan.

"I went looking for them," he whispers. "I wanted to see Kaia and Greta one more time."

"Cal?" Mom asks from behind me. I look over my shoulder at her, then back down at the letter in my hands. "Someone wrote you a letter?"

I nod; "Yes. A friend."

CHAPTER 19

"You cannot be serious."

"I don't understand how you don't like it," I reply with furrowed brows. Cal lifts his head to look up at me with those piercing green eyes.

"Roman," he says. "Roman? As in the fallen empire from...who knows what millennia?"

"It was the first millennia."

"I rest my case! A name from the first millennia of an empire that did not even survive should *not* be the name of our child. That is just solidifying his future falls."

"What? That's absurd. Your name does not dictate who you are to become."

"But why risk it?" he replies with a pensive smirk.

"In some languages, Callum means dove. What future does that solidify for you? You're going to sprout wings and fly off somewhere?"

"I might!" He can't keep the straight face for very long after that response. He laughs into my chest and I can't help laughing with him. He then lifts his head and looks at me again; "My name really means dove?"

"Yep."

"Ugh," he scoffs as he puts his head back down. "We will not name our child something resembling dove. Or any birds for that matter. Can we agree on that part?"

"I don't know, I like Callum. It's a good name."

"We need to be more original than Callum, Junior, though."

"Which is why I suggested Roman."

He sighs painfully in response. I can't fight the grin spreading onto my face.

"So, Prince Callum, with your two-year sentence coming to an end tomorrow, what will you do once you're free?"

I look down at Cal as he chuckles against my chest. We are lying on his bed in his cell beneath Brawnwyn. The bed is meant to hold only one person, so we are entwined to take up as little space as possible. His head on my chest, his torso nestled against my side, and our legs entangled together. At first this was a difficult position to get ourselves into, but after about a week, we discovered the puzzle-like assembly required to fit on the bed. And every night for the past two years, we have contorted ourselves into this exact placement on this bed.

Thankfully, this is the last night we will have to do this. Tomorrow night we will be back in Cal's king-sized bed. Although I have a feeling we will still sleep this close together. I've grown accustomed to it now.

"Other than have sex on a king-sized bed?" he retorts.

I feign a disgusted gasp. "Princes are *not* supposed to speak like that."

He chuckles and kisses my stomach. "Well, in all seriousness, this time has truly given me the opportunity to think about the changes I would like to make once I return to my position as Prince," he answers.

I comb my fingers through his dark blue hair, watching the way it shines in the light above us. "Such as?"

Cal lifts his head and puts his chin on my chest to look up at me. "Helping rebuild the Staxeon village?"

"Really?" That is *not* what I expected.

"Not all of them wanted the uprising. Some of them need help. We should give it to them."

"Last I spoke to Reinhardt and Kaia, things were a lot better. Less discord among them. But I think that's because the majority of the discordant are in jail cells," I reply.

It was only about a week ago that I had met with the happy family. Reinhardt had helped the entire village rebuild to where they were before he was arrested, and things were very close to being back to normal. *It's great to be back with people who think logically,* he had said with his signature smirk. *No more 'Taking back what is ours.' It's time to build our own.*

Kaia couldn't be happier to be able to see her husband outside of a jail cell, which now I understand on an entirely new level. She is the only person who completely understands trying to squeeze onto this small bed. Of course she always makes it her business to remind me that it was three of them fitting in that bed; *And Greta loved to nestle right between us,* she says with an arched eyebrow.

"That's true. But they could still use some help. Financial help. And maybe helping them would make us and our…non-religious government seem a little less overwhelming for them."

I smile at the beautiful, green-eyed man in front of me. "I would very much like to kiss you for that, but I can't bend my head that far," I say as I attempt to crane my neck to no avail.

He laughs and leans toward me, pressing his lips against mine. He pulls away and arches a dark blue eyebrow; "Liking my diplomatic policies, are you?"

"Very much, Your Highness."

He laughs again and places his head back on my chest. A long moment of silence passes between us. I keep gliding my fingers through his silken hair, listening to his breathing and feeling his heart beat against my ribs.

"I love you," I say finally. "You know that, right?"

I can feel his smile against my chest. He lifts his head again to look at me. "I do know that. And I love you. I hope you know that."

"I had an inkling."

"Good," he says as he rests his head down.

I struggle with what to say next. I know what I want to say, but I don't know how Cal will perceive it. I open my mouth and close it repeatedly.

"What?" Cal asks.

I sometimes hate how well he knows me.

"I sometimes…worry about how much you love me. Ugh, no, that isn't right. That's…not…what I mean." Cal lifts his head with a perplexed look on his face. "You would destroy this whole world for me. And you shouldn't."

His eyes narrow. "What are you talking about?"

"I worry about you, Cal. I worry about what would happen to you if anything happened to me."

"What's going to happen to you?" He sits up, taking his feet off the bed.

I sit up. "I'm not immortal, Cal."

"You already promised me that I would die first."

"What? When did I *ever* promise that?"

"Just now. You are promising it right now. I die first. Promise."

I can't stop the giggle that bubbles out of my throat. I shake my head and sigh. When I bring my eyes back up to Cal, he's still looking at me expecting my promise. His jaw is still set and his eyes are pleading; my heart breaks. I place a hand on his face and pull his head to mine. I kiss his lips and his nose before pressing my forehead against his.

"All right," I whisper. "I promise." We kiss again. "Although, it's pretty mean of you to make *me* deal with losing *you*."

"You're far stronger than me, you can handle it," he answers with a smirk.

I scowl at him as I lay back down. A flicker of pain flashes across Cal's face. "You okay?" I ask.

He nods; "Yeah, fine. Just…have a headache." He massages his forehead with the heel of his hand. He yelps and hunches forward. I sit up quickly and take hold of his shoulders.

"Cal? Cal, what's wrong?"

He screams as he grips his head between both hands. Cal collapses to the floor, curling into the fetal position. He grits his teeth, grimacing in pain and letting out this agonizing howl from his throat. My heart is racing and I don't know what to do.

"Help! Someone help! Guard!" I slam on the glass with my fist hoping someone will hear me. "Cal!" I drop to the floor beside him. He's writhing and holding his head with his eyes squeezed shut. Blood trickles from his nose down to his mouth.

"Someone help!" I scream again.

The dull pain above my eyes mutates into a sharp stabbing quickly. I hear a loud beep in my head, as if a bomb went off next to me and has deafened me to only that sound. The pain stretches across my head and down my neck. I grip my head and sink lower to the floor beside Cal. I notice he has gone still. Please don't be dead. He can't be dead. The pain intensifies, the noise grows in volume, and my vision darkens. My body drops to the cold cell floor as the darkness overtakes my vision.

God help us. . .

Help him…

THANK YOU!

Thank you greatly for taking the time to read my book! I hope you enjoyed reading it as much as I enjoyed writing it. Come to think of it, I hope you enjoyed reading it *significantly more* than I enjoyed writing it!

If you truly did enjoy "The Prince", do spread the word to anyone else you think may take as much pleasure in it as you did. If you are interested in reading the next book in the Fenrir Chronicles, feel free to let me know via:

- Facebook (https://www.facebook.com/NaniWrites),
- Twitter (@NanishkaTorres),
- Tumblr (Big Bag of Weird), or wherever you can find me!

I am currently working on the next installment titled "The Soldier". It would be great to know that some people actually *want* it to be released!

A little about me while I have you here: I live in New Jersey, which is causing some of you to cringe. This is the first book I have ever completed and printed, so this is *kind of* a big deal for me! (Woo-hoo!) And I am absolutely addicted to coffee.

The quote at the beginning of the book is from the amazing local (to me) band: Ascending from Ashes. I highly recommend looking them up on YouTube and having a listen to their music. They are the perfect soundtrack while reading "The Prince", working out, or doing just about anything if you enjoy rock/metal music. While I had the idea for this book back in high school, their upcoming album *Glory* (which should be released the fall of 2015) inspired me to actually finish this story.

Thank you all again! And keep an eye out for "The Soldier"!

Book Printed by 48HrBooks
Cover Design by Nanishka Torres

First Edition: June 2015
10 9 8 7 6 5 4 3 2 1